Dance with a Dagger

"Whatcha waitin' fer, cowboy?" he asked. "Let's do it."

The man in the red shirt snatched a bottle, backhanding it against the edge of the table. He held the bottle's jagged edge in the air, and took a step forward.

Stone pulled his knife out of his boot and held it blade up, waving it back and forth like the head of a cobra. Stone's old soldierly fighting spirit came back, and he held the knife tightly in his fist, knowing one of them was going to die.

Red shirt yanked a knife out of its scabbard attached to his belt. They circled each other again, looking for an opening, that one inch that could spell the difference between another glass of whiskey or eternity in a dank, cold grave. . . .

SEARCHER

DEVIL'S BRAND

Josh Edwards

DIAMOND BOOKS, NEW YORK

DEVIL'S BRAND

A Diamond Book / published by arrangement
with the author

PRINTING HISTORY
Diamond edition / November 1991

ISBN: 1-55773-620-0

Diamond Books are published by The Berkley Publishing
Group, 200 Madison Avenue, New York, New York 10016.
The name "DIAMOND" and its logo are trademarks
belonging to Charter Communications, Inc.

PRINTED IN THE UNITED STATES OF AMERICA

10 9 8 7 6 5 4 3 2 1

DEVIL'S BRAND

1

IT WAS NIGHT, and Stone couldn't see anything through the pouring sheets of rain. He was somewhere west of San Antone, and the prairie was a sea of mud and twigs flowing in turbid rivulets toward the Pecos.

He was exhausted and soaked to the skin, drooping on his horse, which plodded stolidly across the puddles, his large round eyes luminescent in the darkness.

The rain had hit that afternoon, after being cloudy all morning and most of the previous night. At first it had been a fine mist, but then became steadier and more intense. By six in the evening it was lashing him like a big black whip in the hand of a giant.

By midnight, he was chilled deep to the bone, and his boots were full of water. He tried to amuse himself by inventing self-baling footwear, and the world would beat a path to his door, only he had no door, only the open prairie and a piece of ground for a bed at night.

He still wore his beat-up old Confederate cavalry officer's hat, but it was little more than a sponge now, and water dripped down his five-day growth of dark blond beard. Sometimes he fell asleep, hunched over the saddle, dreaming he was drowning in a swamp.

He noticed Tomahawk slowing down, and roused himself

1

from slumber as the horse came to a halt in the middle of the pouring rain.

"What's the matter with you?"

The horse stood sullenly in the muck, like a trooper who didn't give a damn anymore. Stone spurred him, but Tomahawk made no reaction. Tomahawk was on his last reserves of energy, and all he wanted to do was sleep.

Stone climbed down to see what was wrong, because it was uncharacteristic of the animal to simply give out. He looked around in the blackness, as rain poured upon his old rawhide leather jacket with fringes that were supposed to leach rain away, but failed miserably.

He walked forward, and then saw it: a stone wall. Tomahawk had stopped because he'd seen the wall and didn't know whether to go right or left. Stone was supposed to be in charge—let him make the decision.

Stone had no idea of where he was. For the last hour or two he'd had the impression they were going around in circles. He couldn't navigate by the stars, and he'd stepped on his compass in a Santa Fe saloon.

A bolt of lightning rent the sky, and for a brief second he saw a rock ledge overhang ten feet away. He pulled Tomahawk toward it, and at that point Tomahawk would go anywhere, even off the edge of a cliff.

They moved beneath the ledge, and it shielded them from the rain, while the mountain blocked the wind. Stone thought it might be a good spot to bed down. He undid the cinch, pulled the saddle off Tomahawk, peeled away the soaking blanket, and lay it against the side of the mountain. He didn't bother tying Tomahawk to anything, because Tomahawk wasn't going anywhere.

Stone unrolled his blanket; it was soaked all the way through. It was going to be a bad night, like the ones during the war when he'd slept in the mud, cannons booming constantly in the distance, but no one would shell him here, and Phil Sheridan wouldn't attack at dawn.

He sat with his back to the wall, twenty-nine years old, his cigarette papers soaked, but he had food and dry matches. If he could find dry wood, maybe he could put his life together again. He crept alongside the mountain, hoping to find an outcropping that protected a few combustible pieces of wood, when he came upon a dark mass that turned out to be the mouth of a cave.

It was four feet wide and four feet high. Stone bent down and looked inside, but it was pitch-blackness. For all he knew, there might be a five-hundred-foot drop just ahead.

He got down on his hands and knees, crawling forward, feeling ahead for the long drop. After several feet he drew himself to his full height, six feet two inches tall. He reached into his shirt pocket, pulled out his waterproof container of matches, unscrewed the lid, and pulled one out.

"Hold it right there," said a deep baritone voice inside the cave. "I got you in my sights."

Stone was so surprised he dropped his matches all over the floor.

"Raise yer hands!"

Stone lifted his arms and faced the voice. "I'm on my way to San Antone, got lost in the rain, and found this cave. I'm not looking for trouble."

"You ain't the law?"

"Hell no. There's probably a few sheriffs who'd like to get their hands on me, though."

"You ain't the only one."

Stone heard the man circle to his back, then felt the barrel of a rifle against his spine. Stone's two Colts were pulled out of their holsters.

"If I'm disturbing you," Stone said. "I'd be happy to move along."

"Sit down."

Stone dropped to the floor cross-legged like an Indian, and wondered what he'd got himself into this time. There was a *scratch* sound, and a match sputtered to life, revealing a bearded, long-haired man wearing a black scarf around his throat, lighting a candle. The wick took fire and glowed, illuminating a cavern with a fireplace against the wall.

"Got a name?"

"John Stone."

"I'm Luke Duvall, and you're the first person what's been in this cave for three years. You'd better not try anythin' funny, because yer life don't mean a damned thing to me."

Stone leaned forward and spread out his hands to show they were empty. "I'm just a drifter on my way to San Antone. I was just looking for a dry spot to lie down."

"That yer hat, or you buy it from some poor old soldier?"

"Mine."

"What outfit were you with?"

"Wade Hampton."

"I served under George Pickett."

Duvall reached across the open space between them, and they shook hands.

"Can't be too careful," Duvall said. "Goddamn territory is full of killers, thieves, and scalp-huntin' injuns." He passed Stone's guns back. "You look like a drowned rat. I'll build the fire."

Duvall moved away, and there was something simian about him, with his hulking shoulders and bowed legs. With flint and steel he set a spark in some shavings, and blew them into a flicker of light. Then he carefully piled twigs around the growing flame, showing a delicacy unexpected in a grizzled beast.

When the large pieces of wood were burning and crackling, Duvall returned to Stone. "Might as well lay yer clothes in front of the fire, and wrap yerself in one of them buffalo robes over there. 'Spect you could use somethin' to eat."

"If it's no bother."

"I ain't much of a cook, tell you that right now."

"You wouldn't happen to have any whiskey around, would you?"

"Haven't touched a drop in three years."

Duvall rustled around the fire, produced a black greasy cast-iron frying pan, and threw a chunk of meat into it. Stone removed his clothes and wrapped himself in a warm fluffy buffalo robe that smelled like fur and leather. Its warmth enveloped him, thawing his frozen bones, and he held his cigarette papers in front of the candle, to dry them out.

"How come you're hiding in this cave?" Stone asked.

"Sick of the world," Duvall replied. "Can't take it anymore."

"Don't you get lonely?"

"People cheat and steal, and send honest men to die."

Stone became aware that Duvall's speech was thick and awkward, as if he weren't accustomed to speaking. The papers were dry now, and Stone rolled a cigarette, lighting it with the candle. "Want some tobacco?"

"Don't smoke, don't use nothin' that ain't absolutely necessary to keep body and soul together. A man searches for the most godforsaken spot he can find, digs in, and next thing he knows some other galoot shows up askin' if he wants a smoke. A man can't escape no matter where he goes."

Stone made a motion to get up. "I'll just leave, if I'm such a bother."

"Now that you're here," Duvall replied, "we might as well make a night of it. What's goin' on out there in the world?"

"You've been here three years?"

"Go to town about once every six months to trade for things I can't git here, like gunpowder and such. Don't spend much time,'cause I don't like it there, but I keep my nose open, to see which way the wind's blowin', if you git my meaning."

"Don't you miss women?"

"It's a woman what put me here."

Duvall handed a tin plate to Stone, and on it were venison and beans with a fork laid on top. Duvall threw a canteen at Stone's feet.

Stone put out his cigarette and dug into the food. "Is there anything for a horse to eat?"

"I'll take care of him," Duvall said. "You just feed your face."

Duvall wrapped himself in a buffalo skin and went outside as Stone wolfed down the food. It had a strange taste, but he was used to trail food, and had eaten many strange things in his day. He looked around at the walls of the cave, now that his eyes were adjusting to the dimness, and saw weird old Indian paintings of horses, warriors, buffalo, coyotes, and snakes.

Then, on the opposite wall, a more sinister painting emerged out of the darkness. It showed a man hanging by his neck at the end of a rope, and the twisted tormented face was a likeness of Luke Duvall.

A chill came over Stone, and he wished he had a drink of whiskey. Duvall returned to the cave, took off his buffalo robe, and threw some logs over the fire. Then Duvall removed his black scarf, hanging it on an outcropping of rock. Stone looked at Duvall's throat and saw the rope scar.

"What you goin' to San Antone for?" Duvall asked.

"Looking for somebody." Stone took a photograph in a silver frame out of his shirt pocket and handed it to him. "Ever see her?"

Duvall held the photograph up to the light and frowned. "Well," he said, "lots of people look alike. What makes you think she's around here?"

"A rancher in Arizona told me he saw her in San Antone, but didn't know her name."

Duvall shrugged. "Hate to bet my life on it, but this looks somethin' like . . . well . . . it's hard to say. What's she to you?"

"We were supposed to be married, but don't be coy, because this is important to me. Who does this person remind you of?"

Duvall gazed into his eyes. "Forget about her."

"I can't forget about her, and don't think I haven't tried."

"The woman I'm thinkin' about is married. Her husband might put a bullet in yer ass."

"I want to find out what happened."

"Never ask a woman what happened, for two reasons. The first is she'll prob'ly lie, so you still won't know—or she'll tell you the truth, and you'll wish you never asked."

"I've got to see her face-to-face," Stone said.

"There was a gal I had to see once," Duvall said. "I should've let her alone, but I pushed it, and wound up on the end of the rope. I know you seen the mark—you keep a-lookin' at it. Well you're liable to get one of these too, if'n you persist after that woman. She belongs to another man."

"She'll have to tell me that, not you, and if she does, I'll just ride away."

"What's the name of the woman you're lookin' for?"

"Marie Higgins."

Duvall shook his head. "Wrong name."

"People change their names. Which one is she using here?"

"Cassandra Whiteside. She's the wife of Gideon Whiteside, and they got a ranch about ten miles southeast of here, the

Triangle Spur. Now you know everythin'. Don't expect me to come to yer funeral."

"I doubt whether there'll be a funeral. I just want to know why she left me."

Duvall shrugged. "Women leave men all the time. You can't trust any of 'em, especially when they look you in the eye and swear to God."

"They're not all that way."

"What I got to go on is my 'sperience, and in my 'sperience, they're a bunch of lyin' polecats—every dang one of 'em."

"Whoever she was, you must still be in love with her, to carry on this way."

Duvall looked down at the floor. "You'd think God would give a man some peace after three years, but I ain't had none yet. I cain't forget her, but she was no good. 'Course, she was young. Only fourteen when I met her."

"Did you kill her?"

"Killed her boyfriend, and that was good enough for the hangman."

"How'd you get away?"

"Maybe the hangman didn't know his job. All I know is I woke up lyin' on a slab in a doctor's office, and had the worst sore throat of my life. I jumped out the window and didn't stop runnin' till I got here, so all I got to tell you is forget that gal and ride on through to somewhere else."

"Wish you had some whiskey."

"The way I see it, whiskey is the downfall of the human race."

Stone looked at the painting of the hanging man flickering in the light of the fireplace. "What did your woman look like?"

Duvall fumbled nervously. "She was a big gal, stronger than most men. Weren't nothin' she couldn't do. Had red hair. God, what kids we would've had, but then she ran off with a rich man, and I killed him."

"You shot him in cold blood?"

"We got in a fight, actually."

"It was self-defense, in other words."

"That's what my lawyer said, but they hung me anyway. Whatever you do, don't shoot a rich man in Georgia."

"You're probably innocent, and there's no need to be hiding

here. Texas is full of men on the dodge, and they're not in caves."

"I got fresh water, all the food I need, God's good clean air, and peace until you showed up. This is my mountain fortress, and I ain't never givin' it up."

"There are gophers who live better than this, Duvall. You should come back to the world, find yourself another woman, plant some potatoes, live like a man."

Duvall shook his head slowly and turned down the corners of his mouth. "Where'll *you* go if that gal tells you to buzz off?"

"Start looking for another gal."

"You can lie to yerself," Duvall said, "but you can't lie to me. You look like a man who'll end up in a cave, but this one's already took. You'll have to find one of yer own."

"You'll never see me in a cave. I love life too much."

"We'll see how much you love life after that little lady tells you to move on. Ever stop to think you're the last person she wants to see right now? I know a nice cave about five mile south of here. Might still be vacant, if you're interested."

2

IT WAS TWO o'clock on the next afternoon, and Stone rode through a sea of cattle grazing in the hot sun. It had been like this for the past three hours, and he figured he was on the range of the Triangle Spur.

For five years he'd searched for Marie, from South Carolina to Kansas, Texas, Arizona, and now was back in Texas again. Here and there men said they'd seen her, sending him on wild goose chases, and in one town an old cowboy lied for a glass of whiskey.

Other veterans were building new lives for themselves, while John Stone roamed the frontier, looking for the only woman he ever loved. She'd lived on the next plantation, and the first time she smiled at him, he felt enveloped in a dazzling radiance. He'd loved her all his life, they were engaged to get married, and then the war broke out.

He rode off to the front, went through five long years of bloody war, and when he returned home, he found Albemarle burned to the ground, his parents dead, and Marie gone. Someone told him she'd headed west with a Union officer, but Stone found that hard to believe. Marie wouldn't go anywhere with a Yankee, at least not the Marie he knew, but he'd come to the frontier looking for her anyway, because he had nothing else to hold on to.

There'd been many temptations along the way, but he'd always been stopped by the memory of Marie. Every town had beautiful women, but there was only one Marie.

Cassandra Whiteside might not be Marie. Sometimes people looked alike, but the rancher in Arizona and Luke Duvall in the cave had said it was her, and maybe it was.

Stone came to the top of a hill, and a broad valley covered with cattle stretched out before him. In the middle of the valley, smoke rising from chimneys, were a complex of buildings, and if Stone's dead reckoning was right, it was the Triangle Spur Ranch.

His heart quickened as he thought Marie might be down there in one of those very buildings. He rode through cattle munching grass, and wondered what he'd do if he saw her. He just couldn't take her in his arms, if she was married to another man. But why'd she marry another man? Too many questions, not enough answers. Soon he'd know it all, maybe.

Rocking back and forth in his saddle, he rolled a cigarette. He'd left tobacco in the cave with Duvall, and Duvall had warned him one last time to forget Marie.

Stone couldn't forget her. A woman could worm her way into your heart, and you'd never get rid of her. He'd been a vagabond for five years, because of Marie.

He approached the farm buildings, and a cowboy shoveled manure into a wagon. Stone leaned over his pommel. "Know where I can find Mrs. Whiteside?"

"In the main house," the cowboy said, pointing his thumb over his shoulder.

Stone rode into the yard that separated the main house from the barn and outbuildings. A tall cottonwood tree sat in the backyard, and a clothesline ran from it to the house. Ladies' underwear hung from the line, next to the clothing of a man, and Stone felt a lump in his throat.

He pulled back Tomahawk's reins, and Tomahawk stopped in front of the ranch house. Tomahawk turned his head and looked at the barn, hoping that's where he'd wind up, in a cool stall with hay and oats, and the possibility for rest.

Stone climbed down from the saddle, threw the butt of his cigarette to the ground, and smoothed the front of his shirt. Then he squared his shoulders and walked toward the front porch. He climbed the stairs, knocked on the door, and there was no answer. He knocked again, and heard light footsteps.

They came closer, and anxiety mounted inside him. The door opened, and he saw a middle-aged woman with graying, thinning hair.

"I'd like to see Mrs. Whiteside," Stone said.

"What about?"

"Just want to see her. It's kind of important."

"Who're you?"

"John Stone, from South Carolina."

The woman looked him over, and he was a mess, his clothes worn and tattered, covered with the dust of the prairie.

"Come in," the woman said. "Have a seat."

Stone entered the living room and saw over the fireplace a huge painting of a man wearing the uniform of the Confederacy, with the rank of colonel on his shoulder straps, his hand resting on his sword. The man had black muttonchop whiskers, and the blue sash around his waist indicated he'd been in the infantry.

The maid disappeared down the hallway, and Stone's insides were quaking. Around him were chairs and a sofa, situated so people could sit near the fireplace. A nice comfortable room, a few cuts above what one would ordinarily find on the frontier.

He heard footsteps approaching in the hallway, and turned toward them. A young blond woman in a light blue dress entered the living room, and Stone took an involuntary step toward her, because *it was Marie!*

He felt as if he were going to have a heart attack, and an expression of alarm came over her face, but then, as she came closer, Stone realized with a second jolt that this woman wasn't Marie, but looked very much like her!

"Are you all right?" she asked. "Would you like to sit down?"

He sank onto a chair and stared at her in disbelief. She was taller than Marie, and Marie's face had been more finely chiseled, but this woman could be Marie's sister, or Marie herself with five more pounds.

"What's wrong?" she asked.

He opened his shirt pocket and showed her the picture. She

took it from his hand. "Why, she looks like me!"

"I thought you were her at first," Stone explained. "I've been looking for this woman for five years. A man in Arizona told me about you, and another man, who lives near here, also told me it was you, but I can see now it's not you, although the resemblance is uncanny."

"You were in love with a woman who looked like me?"

"All my life, practically."

"What happened to her?"

"I have no idea."

"If I'd been her, you would've tried to take me away from my husband?"

"That's right."

"How odd."

"But you're not her, and I'm sorry to bother you." Stone arose, and all he wanted was the nearest saloon. "Good day to you."

He bowed like a southern gentleman, and headed for the door.

"Wait a moment! I want to talk with you about something, and you haven't had tea yet!"

"I could use something a little stronger than tea, ma'am."

"Whiskey?"

"Just what the doctor ordered."

Stone returned to his chair, and she took his hat, hanging it on a peg beside the door. Her figure was similar to Marie's, and he felt like grabbing her, which was probably how Duvall wound up at the southern end of a rope.

The maid arrived with a pot of tea on a tray, setting it on a low table. Cassandra poured a stiff glass of whiskey from a decanter, and handed it to Stone, who raised it to his lips, taking a substantial first swig that sizzled all the way through his innards.

It settled him down, and he leaned back in the chair, staring at Cassandra Whiteside, spotting more differences between her and Marie. This was a rancher's wife, in control of her situation, whereas Marie had been the spoiled daughter of a rich man, and all she ever did was go to parties.

"I imagine you must be very disappointed," Cassandra said. "I'm sorry I'm not the person you seek."

"I was thinking about moving to the nearest cave and not coming out for the rest of my life."

"A handsome fellow like you won't have any trouble finding another girl, I'm sure. Would you need a job by any chance? My husband is hiring men for a cattle drive north to the rails. He's paying thirty dollars a month and your chuck."

"I don't know much about cattle, I'm afraid."

"You can learn on the trail. I can tell by your hat that you were in the cavalry, so you must know horses. Maybe you can be the wrangler, and handle the remuda."

"I'm a little confused right now," Stone said. "I'll have to think about it."

"The drive will begin in ten days. My husband's signed a contract with an eastern broker, and if we don't deliver by October fifth, we're in default. That could be a severe economic blow to this ranch, and maybe the end of it."

"Why did you wait so long to get started?"

"It's taken more time than we thought to gather the herd."

Stone swallowed whiskey, and thought he really didn't have a reason not to take the job. He was down to his last twenty dollars, and would have to find work soon.

"Hate to make a snap decision," he said. "Better run it through my mind." He wasn't sure he wanted to work for a man whose wife looked like Marie.

"Do you have prospects for another job?"

"Nope."

"Then your choice is working for us or working for the Diamond D. Now I can see that you fought for the Confederacy. Well, so did my husband. He left his right arm at Sharpsburg, but the man who owns the Diamond D doesn't care about the Confederacy, he's not even American, he's from Germany, and the D in Diamond D stands for *Deutschland.* Now I've met the gentleman, and have nothing against him personally. In fact, I've found him to be courteous in every way. If you were to work for him, I'm sure you'd find him a fair employer, *but he didn't leave his arm at Sharpsburg.*"

"If I decide to remain in this area," he said, "you can be sure I'll ride for the Triangle Spur. If you don't mind, I'd like to take a walk and think things over."

"If you take the job," Cassandra said, "someday you can tell your grandchildren you went up the trail to Kansas."

"I've heard about John Chisholm's trail," Stone said. "Three hundred miles of Indians, rustlers, tornadoes, stampedes, floods, and folks who don't like Texans."

She smiled faintly. "Exactly."

"A man shouldn't blunder into major enterprises. Got to think it through."

Cassandra gazed at him thoughtfully as he emptied the glass of whiskey. "You must've loved her very much to've come this far."

"Never loved anybody else in my life."

"What was it about her that you loved?"

"The closer to her I got, the better I felt."

"It's different for a woman," Cassandra said. "A man's appearance doesn't mean as much to us. A woman falls in love with a man's mind, and my husband, Colonel Whiteside, is the finest man I ever knew. Since you're a fellow officer, I'm sure he'll want to meet you personally. Why don't you have dinner with us tonight, regardless of your decision? I set my table as fine as anybody in San Antone."

"Be delighted to join you," Stone said, because usually he found himself gnawing on half-cooked meat under open skies.

"The colonel and I look forward to seeing you."

Stone walked out of the house, into the big yard. Tomahawk looked at him hopefully and made a blubber sound with his lips. Stone led him to the barn. Inside was the man who'd been shoveling manure, and now was pitching hay into troughs.

"Can I put my horse in one of these stalls?" Stone asked.

"Help yerself," the man said.

Stone led Tomahawk into an empty stall, took off the saddle and bridle, and fed him hay. Then he walked toward the man, who was examining the hoof of a horse.

"Been working here long?" Stone asked.

The man had a round moon face, and grinned, revealing several missing teeth. "What you want to know fer?"

"I'm thinking about working for Colonel Whiteside."

"Only been here two weeks, but it seems okay. 'Course, I ain't never worked on no ranch before, so I got nothin' to compare it with."

"How's the food?"

"Cook's a little bonkers, but knows his way around a stove, I'll tell you that."

"What's the ramrod like?"

"Knows his stuff."

Stone held out his hand.

"Moose Roykins," the man replied. He was in his early thirties, of medium height, chunky, with pants too big, hanging loose on his hips.

"Boss treat you all right?"

"Colonel Whiteside don't have much to do with the runnin' of the ranch. Ramrod takes care of that. Mrs. Whiteside sure is a purty piece of fluff—you meet her yet?"

"I have."

"What did you think?"

"Not bad."

"Like to git her alone in the hayloft sometime, but to tell you the truth, I prefer an older woman, because they know what it's all about." Roykins giggled and wiped his nose with the back of his hand.

"You going on the cattle drive?"

"Sure am. Why don't you come with us? We'll have a damn good time!"

"Where you from, Roykins?"

"Canada. Used to be a lumberjack." Roykins grinned, and he looked like a big kid.

"Don't reckon you've dealt with Indians and rustlers before?"

Roykins pulled his Colt. "Let the bastards come."

Stone walked out of the barn and found a barrel propped against a well, facing the open range. He sat and rolled a cigarette.

Buffalo grass carpeted the rolling prairie, and clusters of cattle grazed in the sun. In the distance a tall rock formation looked like a pyramid for a long-forgotten pharaoh. He saw cowboys riding among the cattle, and he could be one of them, all the way to Abilene.

The bleak devastation of his soul hit him suddenly like a sledgehammer in the stomach. He'd been following Marie all the way from South Carolina, fighting Indians, drunken cowboys, trigger-happy outlaws, and psychotic lawmen all the way, showing her picture in every town, and it'd been for nothing. He was broke, dressed in rags, a lost wanderer on the face of the earth, and there wasn't even a square foot of land, in all that vast country, that he could call his own.

Cassandra Whiteside had been the last straw. He'd been hoping and praying she'd be Marie, but she wasn't, and his gallant soldier's spirit had finally been defeated by five years of nothing.

He puffed the cigarette and looked at cowboys chasing cattle in the valley. He'd always wanted to learn the ranching business, and this was as good a place as any to start.

He forced himself to remember Marie's defects. She'd do anything to get her way, and threw objects when she got mad. Other women usually didn't like her, and she could be awesome when crossed.

She'd been the most exciting creature he'd ever known, and never failed to thrill him with her touch, but five years of dusty trails and broken-down frontier towns were enough. He was going to forget her and get on with life. The world was full of beautiful women, and someday he'd find one to replace Marie, who'd be even prettier and nicer.

He tried to convince himself of this as he gazed at cowboys riding through great masses of cattle grazing in the sun.

Inside the main house, Cassandra Whiteside sat at her desk in the main office, doing her accounting, but somehow the numbers fuzzed. The experience with John Stone had unnerved her.

The poor man had traveled for years, searching for a woman who looked like her. How peculiar, and almost mystical. She'd never forget the madness in his eyes when he'd first seen her. She'd thought for a moment he was going to attack her, but then disappointment came over his face when he realized she wasn't the woman he sought.

Am I like her? Cassandra wondered. Is there a connection between us, some hidden membrane linking us across time? Do we think alike? Cassandra recalled Stone's weather-beaten features, and he was a southern gentleman through and through.

I don't feel attracted to him myself, Cassandra thought. John

Stone is a mere child compared to my husband.

She tried to convince herself of this as she added up the long columns of numbers.

It was six o'clock in the evening, and Stone approached the front door of the main house, anticipating his first decent meal since leaving Santa Fe. He'd bathed in a stream in the woods, and let the water flow through his clothes. Now they were mostly dry, and he felt reasonably presentable.

He knocked on the door, and the middle-aged maid opened it up. It was obvious that she'd never been a maid before, because she was awkward and nervous, trying to do her best.

"Come on in," she said. "Let me take yer sombrero."

He handed her his hat and entered the living room, gazing at the portrait of Colonel Whiteside above the fireplace. At that moment Cassandra appeared in the hallway.

They looked at each other, and there was an awkward moment, but then she cleared her throat and said, "Well— have you made up your mind?"

"I've decided to sign on."

A broad smile came over her face. "The colonel will be happy to know that. Can I get you a drink?"

"Whiskey, if you please."

"Did you see anything of our spread?"

"Thought it was beautiful."

"It's paradise, except for the Indians and outlaws, but they don't bother us too much here. We're like a small army post. Too many armed men for them to fight."

"How's the cattle business working out?"

"This drive'll make or break us."

"I want to get into the cattle business myself," Stone said. "Don't know how I'll raise the money, but if other people do, so can I."

"Many ranchers started with nothing more than a branding iron and a horse." She handed him a glass of whiskey, and they were close enough to see the colors of each other's eyes, blue all around.

He raised his glass in the air. "To the cattle business."

A deep raspy masculine voice roared into the room. "To hell with the cattle business!"

Stone turned and saw a tall gentleman with graying mutton-chop whiskers enter the room, and he only had his left arm.

"This is John Stone," Cassandra said. "My husband, Colonel Whiteside."

Stone shook the colonel's left hand, noticed the expanse of the colonel's chest, and the colonel was getting a belly. Stone estimated his age in the fifties, while Cassandra was in her early twenties.

"Heard you were in the war," Whiteside said, his eyes glittering with pleasure. "What outfit?"

"Hampton Brigade."

"Fine man, Wade Hampton. What was your rank?"

"Captain."

"I served under General Stonewall Jackson, and of course I was in the infantry. It's my considered opinion that there isn't much use for cavalry in war anymore, but you boys certainly put on a fine show at parades. In the end, however, it's always the infantry, the queen of battle, that decides the ultimate outcome of war. I see you already have a drink. Cassandra, a glass for me, if you please."

Cassandra returned to the bar, and Whiteside sat in front of his portrait. The officer on canvas was trimmer, less gray, more dynamic, and had two arms.

"You toasted the cattle business as I entered the room," Whiteside said. "I'm afraid I can't join you, because the cattle business makes me ill. It's a mundane activity, fattening beasts for the slaughterhouse. I miss the great days of our Cause. Do you?"

"No."

"Surprised to hear you say that. Life's been dull for me since I left the regiment."

Cassandra lowered her eyes, because she'd been with him since he left the regiment.

"What've you been doing since the war?" Whiteside asked Stone.

"Drifting and drinking."

"You're with the Triangle Spur now, and your life has purpose again. You're going up the trail to Kansas, and by Christ, I wish I could go with you, but I have to stay with my wife."

"Bring her along," Stone said. "I've heard of women going up the trail with the men."

"Wouldn't want to expose her to the danger. It's not for a woman. Were you at Sharpsburg, by any chance?"

"Afraid so."

Cassandra compared them as they discussed the battle of Sharpsburg. Stone was a vital young animal, with tanned good looks and shaggy dark blond hair, while her husband was a lofty intelligence. He'd done magnificent things, he had the profile of a king, with long, wavy, graying hair sweeping over his leonine head.

The maid entered the parlor. "Dinner is served."

They walked toward the hall, and Whiteside placed his arm around Stone's shoulder. "It's good to see another officer. One feels isolated out here. Most of the people we meet are quite primitive. Did you go to West Point?"

"Unfortunately."

"I never did, but I guess you knew that. You West Point fellows are a brotherhood I was never privileged to join. Didn't you like West Point?"

"I learned a lot I had to forget."

They came to a small dining room, with four chairs. Cassandra motioned to one of them, and Stone took his position behind it. On the far wall hung a painting of Stonewall Jackson on a horse, with a Confederate flag fluttering behind him.

Whiteside noticed Stone looking at the portrait. "That's the man I fought for," Whiteside said. "Ever meet him?"

"Once."

Whiteside puffed up his chest. "General Jackson was the finest man I ever met, and in my opinion one of the greatest field commanders in the history of warfare. You ever study the Shenandoah Valley Campaign? I was there when General Jackson said, 'If this valley is lost, Virginia is lost, and if Virginia is lost, the Confederacy is lost.' So the proud old foot cavalry fought Yankees from Harrisburg to the Blue Ridge Mountains, in a series of battles that are pored over by the scholars and historians to this day, and we beat the shit out of the Yankees. They couldn't even find us most of the time. Your glass is empty. Agnes!"

The maid appeared in the doorway.

"Set the bottle on the table, and hurry with the dinner will you? My wife is hungry." Whiteside filled Stone's glass, then his own. "By God, it's good to be with a fellow officer again. I feel like a fish out of water here."

"Where are you from?"

"Virginia originally, and then New Orleans. The disease called *Reconstruction* took all the pleasure out of life, so we came to Texas, and it's better than the Yankee and nigra-dominated South of today, but it's not much compared to Old Dixie. Cassandra told me you're from South Carolina. What did your family do?"

"We were planters."

"You must've known Wade Hampton personally, then."

"We were neighbors."

"Then you know he never went to West Point either, never commanded troops in his life, and knew nothing of war, but became an outstanding officer, isn't that so?"

"Some of us thought he was better than Jeb Stuart."

"My point exactly. You don't have to go to West Point to learn war, and in fact, maybe you can't learn it at all. Perhaps you must be born with it. What do you think?"

"Right now, all I'm interested in is the cattle business."

"The main thing you've got to do in the cattle business is hire a good foreman and let him take care of everything. It's not a very edifying enterprise, let me tell you. The cattle eat all day long, and when they're fat you send them to the butcher. No grand strategies are required, no noble acts of courage, no brilliant tactical concepts. It's sad, but old soldiers such as we have to go on living somehow."

Agnes entered the room with a tureen of soup, and placed it on the table. Cassandra took the ladle and poured soup into her husband's bowl, then Stone's, and when her eyes met Stone's, she thought: *When he looks at me, he thinks of the woman he loved all his life.*

"I'd like to change places with you," Whiteside said to Stone. "If I were your age, and had my other flipper back, I'd return to the service. It's the only life for a man, in my opinion. I don't want to pry, but can't help being curious—why didn't you return?"

"Got tired of soldiering."

"How can anyone get tired of it? It was something new every day, and I felt as if my life had great purpose!"

Stone said nothing as he dipped into chicken consommé. He wondered how a man who lost an arm at Sharpsburg could be so enthusiastic about war.

"The best part of it," Whiteside continued, "was the wonderful men I met. I'm not ashamed to say that I was a great admirer of General Jackson. He truly was a stonewall, unshakable and indomitable at all times, even in the worse circumstances. Yet he was a God-fearing man, moderate in his habits, modest in demeanor, quite unlike your Jeb Stuart, who wore peacock plumes in his hat and sang songs with his staff. General Jackson was no singer of songs."

Again, Stone didn't respond. He recalled being presented to General Jackson en masse with the other officers of Wade Hampton's command, shortly before Second Manassas. General Jackson had the aura of command, and was correct in every movement he made. He listened carefully to what was said, and had been especially friendly to the younger officers like Stone. General Jackson had spoken of the importance of receiving accurate up-to-date intelligence information, and said he was counting on his cavalry to provide it. Many of General Jackson's senior commanders had attended the gathering, but Stone didn't recall Colonel Whiteside. Maybe the colonel had been on duty that night.

The colonel said, "We may be brother officers, but my ramrod treats all the men alike. Duke Truscott is a hard man, let me tell you. I hope my wife hasn't given you the impression that you'll have an easy time of it here. After this evening, you'll eat with the men. That won't be as onerous as you might think, because they've got an extremely fine cook. He's a nigra, but hand him a piece of anything edible, and he'll turn it into the most delicious meal you ever ate. I'd like to bring him into my own kitchen, but I think my cowboys would quit if I did."

Agnes cleared away bowls and the tureen, then returned with a platter covered with a silver dome, which she placed in front of Whiteside.

He removed the dome, revealing a leg of lamb swimming in gravy, garnished with potatoes and okra. Taking the carving knife in his one good hand, he sawed thick slices off it.

"We're still shorthanded for the drive," Colonel Whiteside said. "If you know anybody who might be looking for a job, I'd appreciate it if you'd steer him in this direction. We need more men, and I don't know where they're going to come from because we're scraping the bottom of the barrel as it is."

Stone flashed on Luke Duvall in the cave. "I have a friend, but he's unusual."

"It what way?"

"Not very friendly."

Whiteside leaned back in his chair and laid down the knife. "There's nothing wrong with being discriminating in our choices of friends. I, for one, do not tolerate fools either."

Cassandra filled Stone's plate and handed it to him. "We desperately need cowboys," she said. "We'd appreciate it if you'd tell your friend about us."

"I'll see him tomorrow, if that's all right with you."

"By all means."

Their eyes met, held for a few seconds, then ran away. She cut her husband's meat into small pieces, while he sipped his whiskey.

Whiteside leaned forward and declared, "I think courage is the most important quality a man can have, and what is courage? Nothing more, in my opinion, than holding steady under fire. That I saw at Sharpsburg, and it was the supreme moment of my life. Men were shot down all around me, and I myself was severely wounded, but my regiment held their ground, not one man broke and ran."

Stone listened politely, but he'd never been in a battle where somebody didn't break and run. Sometimes even battle-hardened veterans cracked under the strain of long bombardment, and Stone himself had been through numerous tight situations where he thought he wasn't going to make it. Maybe he would've run too, if he hadn't commanded old Troop C, and the men depended on him.

Colonel Whiteside continued to talk about Sharpsburg, while Cassandra studied them both, a faint smile on her face. Her husband was a grand gentleman, and his every gesture bespoke breeding and character, while Stone was withdrawn, gloomy, and smoldering with a deep intensity. He seemed almost like an infant compared to her husband, but she supposed there were superficial women who'd prefer Stone only because he was youthful and melancholy, a lost wandering poet.

Stone's mind was wandering, he didn't like to talk about the war. It reminded him of too many dead friends, too much suffering, all that futility, and the lost paradise his youth had been. Something made him glance toward Cassandra, and their eyes met once more. For a millisecond he thought she was Marie, and made a motion toward her, then checked himself and returned to his lamb.

It was uncanny to have her sitting there, looking so much like Marie, but she was another man's wife, and he had to stop thinking about her. Fortunately he wouldn't see her much after this meal. He'd be in the bunkhouse, riding for the brand, and he'd rather be a cowboy in Texas than an officer at Sharpsburg any day.

"There's something I'd like to show you," Whiteside said. He pushed his chair back, arose from the table, and walked out of the dining room.

Cassandra turned to Stone. "I hope you're enjoying your meal."

"If the cook in the bunkhouse is better than this, he must be spectacular."

"I don't think you'll have any complaints. Is it unsettling for you to sit with a woman who looks like the one you were supposed to marry?"

"Does it show?"

"Sometimes when you look at me, I think you're looking at her, and it unnerves me, because I start imagining I'm her. Do I really look much like her?"

"The resemblance is amazing."

"Do I behave like her? Is my voice like hers?"

"Let's just say it's too close for comfort."

"I hope I'm not causing you any distress. I don't mean to."

"On the contrary, I don't want to make you uncomfortable at your own table."

She placed her hand on his arm. "You must never be false, not to me, not to anyone. I can take care of myself, so relax, we're happy to have you with us for dinner."

Whiteside returned to the dining room with a box made from

handworked Spanish leather. He opened it, and inside was an arrangement of medals displayed against purple velvet.

"I'm not ashamed to say," Whiteside told Stone, "that these are my most valuable possessions. I realize I may appear foolish, and a bit vainglorious, the vestige of an era long past, but I'm proud to say I belonged to the old Stonewall Brigade, I stood steady with it at Sharpsburg, and that's the highest honor that can come to any man!"

Stone looked at the medals, and they were the usual ribbons and tin junk they gave you if you were there and somehow survived, and if you didn't survive, they sent the whole clanking mess to your mother.

"I imagine you must have medals of your own that you treasure," Whiteside said, returning to his seat, leaving the display case open beside him. "Would you like to get them?"

"Don't have them anymore."

"What happened?"

"Traded them for a bag of groceries."

Whiteside turned purple. "You gave up your medals for one bag of groceries!"

"The man said that's all they were worth."

"You should've shot him!"

"I was mainly interested in the groceries."

Whiteside stared at him in horror, then an expression of sympathy came over his face. "I've run into men like you, demoralized by our defeat, but just remember we old soldiers must always remain brothers no matter what our circumstances become. When you go to the bunkhouse, and become one of my cowboys, we'll still be comrades in arms, and if you ever feel the need to speak with me about anything, don't hesitate to knock on my door."

Dinner was over, and Cassandra watched her husband and their new hand make their way through the moonlit darkness toward Truscott's cabin. She stood at the dining-room window, a cup of tea in her fingers, wondering about the woman John Stone had followed. What must she've been like, to have a man so much in love with her?

Cassandra wished she knew some of her tricks, because her husband wasn't that affectionate. If he had his choice, he'd rather shoot the breeze with other ex-soldiers, and she accepted that, as long as she could be part of his life.

John Stone had his charms, but he didn't have the greatness of Colonel Gideon Whiteside. Stone had been sullen and withdrawn throughout the meal, although sometimes he'd said something pointed, or made a wry observation. He'd been respectful to her husband, deferring to him as a junior commander would to his senior, but it was obvious that Stone thought her husband a blowhard. It was true that Gideon was rather grand in his mode of expression, but he was no blowhard.

She watched as they walked side by side across the yard, and Stone towered over her husband. Stone had wide shoulders and looked solidly packed; he must've been spectacular in his uniform. Too bad he'd become a morose young man, but that was part of his immaturity. A real man like her husband would be constant in his temperament regardless of outer circumstances, and that's why they'd given him a regiment in the Stonewall Brigade, whereas John Stone only led a troop of cavalry, just another captain, quite a low rank without nearly as much responsibility.

When Stone looked at her during dinner, she felt uneasy. Now alone, she hugged herself and laughed softly, because it was so amusing. She looked like the woman he loved, and both of them were becoming spooked. It was like a game, or the ingredients for a French farce. Sometimes she imagined she was the woman, and sometimes Stone thought she was too, to judge by the passion that came into his eyes during those moments.

She saw them stop at Truscott's cabin, and her husband knocked on the door. A few moments later the door opened, and then Truscott put on his hat and came outside.

Stone looked at Duke Truscott in the light of the moon, and read him as a tough son of a bitch. He had a thick brown mustache that drooped down at the ends, and his jaw looked as if it had been carved out of granite. His skin was deeply tanned, he was around forty years old, and whiskey was on his breath.

"I'd like to introduce you to our new hand," Whiteside said to Truscott. "This is John Stone, and he was with the cavalry during the war."

Truscott looked Stone up and down. "You ever work cattle?"

"No."

Truscott turned to Whiteside. "How d'you expect me to take this herd to Kansas with a crew of inexperienced men?"

"You'll have to teach them what they need to know. Captain Stone here is skilled with horses. Perhaps he can handle the remuda."

"We've already got a wrangler. This man'll ride the drag."

"Whatever you say." Whiteside shook Stone's hand. "The best of luck to you. If you ever want to talk, just knock on my door."

Colonel Whiteside walked back to the house, and Stone saw Cassandra standing behind the dining-room window.

"Let's understand each other from the get-go," Truscott said to Stone. "I don't care what you did in the war, and I don't care if you're Whiteside's long-lost brother from New Orleans, you work for me—you do what I say. Get it?"

"Yes, sir."

"I'm a fair man, or at least I try to be, but a man gives me trouble, I'll fire him on the spot, and I don't care if it's in the middle of Indian Territory. Go to the bunkhouse and report to the *segundo*. Any questions?"

"Colonel Whiteside said I could take tomorrow off, because I have a friend who might want to sign up."

"He got any 'sperience with cattle?"

"Not that I know of."

"Jesus Christ!" Truscott spat into the dust. "I never seen such a screwed-up outfit in my life!"

"Why do you stay?"

Truscott looked at him, narrowing his eyes. "My personal life is none of yer goddamned business. I told you to report to the *segundo*. Get goin'."

Stone tipped his hat, then strolled toward the bunkhouse. He figured there weren't many foreman jobs available, and Truscott had to take what he could get.

Stone came to the bunkhouse, and a group of men sat around a table, playing cards. Others lay on their bunks, reading old worn-out magazines in the dim light of the lantern. One young man sat on his footlocker, repairing a bridle.

"Who's the *segundo*?" Stone asked.

"Who wants to know?" asked a heavyset man with grizzled jowls and thick lips.

"My name's John Stone, and I've just been hired."

The man stood, and he wasn't wearing a shirt. Thick slabs of muscle covered his torso, and the mangy cur sitting next to him arose and growled softly at Stone.

"I'm the *segundo*," he said. "Name's Braswell. Take any empty bunk. You eat yet?"

"Yep."

"Know anything about cattle?"

"Nope."

"'At's what I figgered." The *segundo* introduced Stone around the bunkhouse, and Stone knew he'd never remember all the names. Finally they came to the Canadian lumberjack.

"We've met," Stone said.

Moose Roykins shook his hand happily. "We'll have a damn good time!"

A Negro tall as Stone emerged through the back door.

"This is our cook," the *segundo* said. "Ephraim's his name, and he may be a nigra, but he knows his grits."

Stone looked at Ephraim, and felt ill at ease. Stone's family had owned slaves before the war, and it was difficult for Stone to regard them as free men, with the same rights and privileges as he.

Ephraim gazed at Stone, and at first it appeared that Ephraim didn't like what he saw, but then Ephraim grinned and held out his hand. "Howdy."

Stone hesitated a moment, then shook hands with him. "Howdy."

The dog at the *segundo*'s feet growled, and the *segundo* kicked him halfway across the room. "I toldja to shut up, you damned flea-bitten son of a whore!" Then he turned to Stone and said, "We rise at dawn, and tomorrow we're doin' what we been doin' for the past month, formin' up the herd, but I don't suppose you know anything about that."

"No."

"It's the sort've thing you either learn—or it kills you." The *segundo* laughed. "Hey—you're the feller what had supper with the boss lady, ay?"

"That's right."

Braswell winked. "Pretty little filly, ain't she?"

"I'll guess they're all pretty when you spend most of your life with cattle."

"Shore like to git her out on the prairie one of these nights." Braswell balled up his fists, closed his eyes, and shook his hips lewdly. "I'd show her what a real man can do."

"Where's the real man?" asked Moose Roykins.

A string bean of a man picked up a guitar and sang:

"Listen to me, waddies
and I'll tell you a tale
'bout whiskey and whores
on the old Chisholm Trail . . ."

Stone thought he'd better check Tomahawk, then get his saddlebags. He wanted to go to bed early, so he could rise at dawn and ride to Duvall's cave.

He stood in the moonlight and rolled a cigarette. It had been pretty much like a barracks in the bunkhouse, and Braswell was the sergeant. The only difference was that Stone had never slept in the barracks with the men. He'd gone home at night to the Bachelor Officers' Quarters, and enjoyed the company of gentlemen such as himself.

That had been before the war, when all had been spit and polish. Then the shooting started, and he found himself spending most of the next five years on the ground with his men, and they turned out to be more interesting, in their own way, than gentlemen.

He passed the main house, and lights shone through its second-floor windows. He thought of Cassandra and Colonel Whiteside in bed, and it made him wince.

He entered the barn and found Tomahawk in his stall. Tomahawk looked at him dolefully and hoped he wouldn't have to carry Stone around all night.

"Hello, old boy, how they treating you? Get enough to eat?"

Stone looked in the trough, saw hay and oats mixed with molasses. The stall was clean, and Tomahawk seemed strangely subdued. Maybe it was the molasses, because he usually didn't get that rare delicacy. Maybe it had upset his stomach.

"See you tomorrow morning, fellow," Stone said, patting Tomahawk's nose, then he turned away, heading for the door, and Tomahawk breathed a sigh of relief.

Stone rolled a cigarette. The day was coming to an end, his dream was over, and it was time for a new dream. I'll be a cattle king.

Something moved to his right behind the stalls. Stone dropped his cigarette paper and tobacco and pulled out both Colts, cocked them, and prepared to fire.

Ephraim, the Negro cook, stepped out of the shadows. "Hello, Massa John, don't you reckernize me?"

"Have we met?" Stone asked.

"We ain't never been introduced before today, but I knows you, Massa John."

Stone examined Ephraim's strong African features. "Afraid I don't remember."

"Guess you had other thangs on yer mind, since you was up there on the porch with yer friends, drinkin' mint julep, and I was down in the fields, with my mother and my brother, pickin' yer father's fuckin' *cotton!*"

Ephraim said the last word with such vehemence that he startled Stone, and Stone took a step back. Stone recalled those sultry afternoons on the back porch, discussing the great questions of the day with his friends, and before him the fields were covered with slaves, and one of them had been Ephraim.

Stone looked him in the eye. "That's over and done with, but if you want to do something, make your move."

Ephraim smirked. "It must hurt, havin' to deal with a man who was once yer property, who you think ain't as good as you, ain't that right, Massa John?"

"Maybe."

Ephraim suddenly dropped into a fighting stance; he looked like a panther in the moonlight. "You want to tussle, Massa John?"

"Up to you."

"How did you like the war, Massa John?"

"About as much as I like you."

"I used to see you in yer uniform, and you looked real fine,

Massa John, all the pretty gals hangin' around you. I used to
wish I was you, and sometimes I asked God why I couldn't've
been borned in yer boots, and you in mine, so's I could have
all the fun with the pretty girls, and you could see what hell
was like on yer hands and knees in the fields."

Stone had known a slave's life was hard, and was aware of
the Abolitionist and moral arguments. Like Robert E. Lee and
many other southerners, he hadn't believed much in slavery,
but fought to save the South from the Yankee invader.

Stone looked at him evenly. "If you think you can make
everything right by fighting me, do it. Otherwise get out of
my way."

Ephraim didn't budge. "I'd kick yer sickly white ass all
over this barn, but then they'd lynch me, and I'm too young
to die. I'm a-gonna handle you another way, Massa John. I'm
the cook on this cattle drive, and whatever you eat will pass
through these two big nigra hands." Ephraim held them up so
Stone could see the palms. "If I was you, I'd go over to the
Diamond D right now, and forget this spread."

Stone pointed both his guns at Ephraim. "If I ever taste
anything funny in my food, I'm coming after you, and you
won't be the first man I've killed."

Ephraim smiled bitterly. "You're real brave, with all the
laws and sheriffs and judges behind you, but someday we're
gonna be alone, and the time's gonna be right, and maybe den
we'll git it on, you and me."

"Just say when," Stone said.

Ephraim winked. "You know, they say a cook can make or
break a man on a cattle drive."

Ephraim hunched himself over and pretended to be an old
Negro slave shuffling out of the barn. When he reached the
exit, he raised himself to his normal posture and crossed the
yard, swinging his arms like a confident free man in full
possession of his powers. Stone knew if he ever got into it
with Ephraim, it'd be a gruesome bloody fight to the death.

Stone adjusted the saddlebags on his shoulder, rolled a cigarette, and strolled out of the barn. The lamp still glowed in the
second-floor window, and again Stone thought of Whiteside
and Cassandra in bed. Stone wondered why, no matter what
he did, things got worse. It was as though he was jinxed, but if

he left the Triangle Spur now, Ephraim would think he'd been afraid.

If I could get through five years of war, I can get through this cattle drive. If the food's lousy, it was lousy in the army too, and it didn't kill me.

He entered the bunkhouse, and a few cowboys drank whiskey at the table, their faces golden in the light of the lamp. Stone walked to the rear of the bunkhouse, and saw the *segundo* lying on his bunk, his arms wrapped around his dog, and both were sleeping.

Stone found an empty bunk in a dark corner and threw his bedroll upon it. He dropped onto the bunk and closed his eyes, thinking about Ephraim, Cassandra, Marie, and Whiteside. *Maybe I should've moved into that cave*, he thought as he drifted away.

3

LUKE DUVALL SAT on a buffalo robe in the middle of his cave, weaving a rope out of rawhide. "You give a man a meal," he said, "and you talk with him awhile, and you never see the end of him."

Stone stood at the entrance to the cave, a pint of whiskey in his hand. "Thought I owed you a drink for taking me in out of the rain, and besides, I've come to make you an offer."

"If I had a wallet, I'd hide it about now, but since I don't, I guess I don't got nothin' to worry about. Pull up a piece of the floor and sit yer ass down. Until you came along, nothing ever crawled into this cave except a badger and a polecat, but now I guess I you're gonna hound me till my dyin' day, and I don't even owe you no money."

Stone uncorked the bottle, and it was half full. His eyes were glassy and his face was red. He drank some of the whiskey and passed the bottle to Duvall.

"One won't kill you."

"It never ends with one, and you know it." Duvall stroked his beard as he examined Stone. "Let me guess. The woman you was supposed to marry didn't even reckernize you, and when you told her who you was, she told you to take a flyin' fuck at the moon."

"It wasn't the same woman."

"Don't blame it on me. Told you a man couldn't be sure.

33

Anyways, I figgered you'd end up back here. Took one look at you and said to myself: *That man's gonna wind up in a cave,* but I didn't realize it'd be *my* cave."

"You've got it wrong—I'm going up the trail to Abilene, and *you're coming with me!*"

Duvall shook his head emphatically. "I ain't leavin' my mountain stronghold."

"You call this rathole a mountain stronghold? You ought to be ashamed of yourself, hiding from the world like this. Let's go to Kansas, for crying out loud, and if we're lucky, maybe the Comanches'll kill us."

"Good point," Duvall said, raising his forefinger. "If we go out on that there cattle drive, there's the strong possibility we'll stop somebody's arrow or bullet, and all our worries will be over."

Stone leaned toward him. "They need cowboys at the Triangle Spur, and the boss himself told me they're scraping the bottom of the barrel. That means men like us can get hired. We can learn the cattle business, Duvall, and who knows, maybe if we're really unlucky, and make it all the way to Abilene, we can go to one of those fancy whorehouses. It won't be love—but it'll do until love comes along, and who knows if love exists anyway, do you?"

"I know that likker has gone to yer damn fool head." Duvall pushed the bottle away. "Got to keep my mind clear."

"For what? You're like a man in a coffin, you might as well be dead. So what if they tried to lynch you in Georgia? Better men than you have been lynched. Hell, once even *I* nearly got lynched. Have a drink, for Christ's sake. You've forgotten how to have fun."

"I don't see where there's any fun in a bottle."

"I rode all the way out here for nothing," Stone said with disgust. "You're a dried-up old fart, and I shouldn't've wasted my time. I could be in a saloon in San Antone right now, watching the girls dance, instead of sitting with you in this stinking damned hole in the wall. Give me my bottle! I wouldn't trust a man who wouldn't drink with me!"

Stone reached for the bottle, but Duvall pulled it out of his reach and tossed it over his shoulder. Stone watched in stark horror as the bottle sailed across the cave and smashed against the wall next to an Indian painting of a girl riding a wild raging bull.

"I know who you are!" Duvall said, staring fixedly at Stone. "You're the devil, here to tempt me with the pleasures of the flesh!"

"I'm not the devil," Stone replied, "and you sure as hell aren't Jesus. You owe me a goddamned bottle of whiskey." Stone jumped to his feet, yanked out his guns, and aimed them at Duvall. "On your horse!"

"Now just a goddamned minute!"

"Get moving, or you'll *really* need a coffin!"

Duvall shook his head sadly. "Try to hide from the world, and one of the bastards will always find you. There's no gittin' away from 'em. Lord, where did I go wrong?"

Stone was reeling drunk in the middle of the cave, brandishing both his Colts. "You owe me a bottle of whiskey, and you're going to pay me back, you hairy old muskrat!"

"I ain't got no money!"

"You'll work for it as a dish washer, or a floor sweeper, or you'll be the galoot who empties the cuspidors!" Then suddenly Stone realized he had both guns out and was raving like a maniac. "Sorry," he muttered. "Haven't been right since I saw that Whiteside woman."

Duvall reached over, pulled his shotgun from underneath a buffalo robe, and lay the shotgun on his lap. "You pull them guns again, you'll find yerself in a war worse than the last one you was in."

"I just want to get you out of this cave. It's not a natural life. I thought we could go to Abilene together and forget the women who've ruined us. We could start over again, become ranchers together."

"We ain't got no money, and I ain't leavin' this cave."

"You mean to say you don't want to see dancing girls, and you won't have a drink with me?"

"You got it."

"Sorry I bothered you. You can rot in hell, for all I care."

Stone got to his feet and walked unsteadily out of the cave. Tomahawk stood underneath the ledge, wondering where the fool wanted to go next. Stone tightened the cinch, and heard a footfall behind him.

It was Duvall emerging from the cave, his skin pale as snow in the sunlight. "Wait for me."

"What for?"

Duvall looked down at his boots like a naughty little boy. "Might be fun to see some dancin' girls. Gits lonely here sometimes."

Duvall left to get his horse, and Stone had the mad urge to return to the cave and lick the whiskey off the wall. He realized he'd been thinking and behaving erratically ever since he found out Cassandra Whiteside wasn't Marie, and he'd have to get hold of himself. *If I keep on like this, I'll end up dead.*

Duvall returned with his horse, a mustang he'd caught and broken himself, and the mustang looked forlornly at Tomahawk, his eyes saying: They got you too, huh?

Duvall hesitated. "I don't know if I'm doin' the right thing."

"Don't think about it," Stone said. "Just get on your horse and follow me."

"Sometimes when I drink, I gits a little crazy."

"We all do."

Duvall looked confused and defeated as he hoisted himself atop his saddle. "Lead the way," he said to Stone.

Stone touched his spurs to Tomahawk's withers, and the big black horse began the long walk toward the famous fabled streets of San Antone.

It was afternoon at the Triangle Spur Ranch, and Cassandra was bent over her desk. She managed the ranch administratively, and there were so many records to keep, bills to pay, letters to write, arrangements to make.

When Truscott went up the trail, he'd have a letter of credit good anywhere, and that required a substantial deposit, but the Triangle Spur was low on funds. Cassandra had put her entire inheritance into the operation, and if they didn't earn a decent profit on the drive, she'd be wiped out.

Gideon didn't know anything about ranching, but you couldn't expect a man of his caliber to pollute his mind with everyday commerce. He was a visionary, and his noble profile belonged on a coin or a statue. He would've been a great president or senator, but his seigneurial spirit had no space for the double-dealing and deception required by smoky back-room politics.

She'd met him at a church service, and he'd been modest at first; you'd never know he was a war hero. She'd been put off by his age, but gradually became drawn to that fine aristocratic profile, his proud spirit. And now they were married, forging a new future for themselves on the frontier, if they didn't go broke first.

She heard footsteps in the hallway, and moments later the colonel entered, dropping onto the sofa, lying his head back, and stretching out with a groan.

"What's wrong?" she asked.

"Feel sick," he said. "That John Stone fellow did it to me. He can't help being what he is, but he lacks that magic spark, know what I mean? No, you probably don't, because you've never lived at the front, with shells crashing around you and bullets flying through the air thick as mosquitoes on the bayou. The man fought for something decent and fine. He tasted glory and even was introduced to General Jackson, but now it means nothing to him. All he wants to do is raise cattle. Some people have no imagination. They're numb in their souls, Cassandra, more like animals than men. What are you doing?"

"The books."

"You spend so much time with them. How are we doing?"

"Not so well."

"Don't you have a relative who could help out?"

"Afraid not."

"We'll make do. How did I ever end up in this godforsaken Texas?"

"It was your idea to come here, but I'm sure everything will turn out just as we planned, once we get the herd to Abilene. Then we'll have a big celebration, just the both of us, all right?"

Whiteside's eyes brightened. "Nothing like a big town, is there, Cassandra? Do you remember New Orleans?"

She recalled the hotel room where they'd spent days and nights drinking champagne and making love. Lying her pencil on the desk, she arose from her chair and knelt before him, resting her cheek on his lap.

"Not now, dear," he said, pushing her away. "I'm not feeling well. I hope John Stone doesn't accept my invitation and come knocking on my door one of these nights. I find him insufferable. If he ever comes looking for me, tell him I'm out, will you?"

John Stone had sobered up by the time they hit San Antone, and Duvall had the eyes of a terrified squirrel as they rode down the city's main street, full of carriages, wagons, men on horseback, dogs, children, and even a goat tied to the rear of a covered wagon parked in front of the Last Chance Saloon.

"Looks like a good place to start," Stone said.

He angled Tomahawk's head to the curb, and Tomahawk knew from long experience what his afternoon was going to be: hang out with the other horses in front of the saloon, wait for his boss to return unsteady and unsure, and they'd wander off into the prairie for a night under the stars.

Stone climbed down from the saddle and threw the reins over the rail. He loosened the cinch and patted Tomahawk's thick black mane. "Take it easy, and I'll be back in a while. Don't bite anybody, and don't stomp any kids."

Duvall sat on his horse, his lips quivering with fear. The sidewalk was crowded with cowboys, businessmen, gamblers, Mexicans wearing wide sombreros, whores, and he saw a wanted poster nailed on a wall.

Stone grabbed his shirt and dragged him to the ground. "Be a man," he said. "It's only a goddamned saloon."

"I ain't been in one in three years."

"I'd be ashamed to admit it, if I were you. It's a sad commentary."

Stone held his shirt and pulled him onto the sidewalk, through the crowd, and into the Last Chance Saloon, a long rectangular room with a bar to the left, tables to the right, and above the bar a painting of three naked women cavorting in a meadow dotted with flowers.

It was crowded with men in suits, cowboys outfits, and everything in between. Women in low-cut dresses worked the floor, delivering drinks, sitting with the men, accompanying them upstairs to the private rooms. In back, through clouds of tobacco smoke, were roulette wheels and monte games, and somebody hollered: " 'Round and 'round she goes, and where she stops, nobody knows!"

Stone and Duvall bellied up to the bar, and Duvall looked as though he were going to faint. His eyes rolled around in his head like two loaded dice, and he licked his lower lip nervously. His shirt was buttoned to the top, so the rope scar wouldn't show.

The bartender, a short mustachioed Mexican in a white shirt, stopped in front of them. "Your pleasure, señor?"

"Two whiskeys, and do you have dancing girls?"

"The next show starts in an hour."

"I don't see the stage."

"There is none." The bartender dropped two wet glasses on the bar and filled them with amber fluid, then moved down the bar to a slender man wearing glasses and a suit, who looked like a professor.

"How're you doing?" Stone asked Duvall.

"Not so good."

Stone raised his glass in the air. "To the dancing girls!"

He raised the glass to his lips and drank off the top, savoring the hickory flavor, the smooth bouquet, and then it hit, rotgut frontier whiskey that could take paint off wood.

Duvall stared at his glass, fighting with himself. One side said go to your cave and meditate, and the other said drink it down, what the hell are you afraid of? Duvall sighed, sucked wind through clenched teeth, and opened his mouth, pouring the entire glass down his throat.

He wiped his mouth with the back of his hand, placed the glass on the bar, and his face turned red as a beet. He coughed a few times, swallowed, then turned to Stone. "I don't know who you are, or what purpose you have in my life, but it looks like a night of hard drinkin'."

Stone reached toward him, and they shook hands. Then Stone drained his glass and called the bartender again. "Two more whiskeys, governor, when you've got time!"

Duvall hadn't touched a drop in three years, and already the room was rocking. He gazed through the smoke and saw gamblers, freighters, drunken cowboys, horse traders, bankers talking deals, Mexican vaqueros with guns and knives, but somehow it didn't seem so threatening now. A woman bent over a table in front of him, and he admired her hindquarters. An old urge came over him, an urge he'd thought he'd conquered, but it was insistent and unsettling, and he became afraid.

"What's wrong?" Stone asked.

"That woman . . ."

Stone reached into his pocket and took out all the money he had. "You want her—take her. On me. Don't deprive yourself. It's not worth it."

Duvall stared at the woman, a buxom redhead with freckles on her shoulders, and a hefty bottom a man could use to anchor his most ambitious efforts.

"Go ahead," Stone said. "Every man needs to stand on that mountain once in a while."

"How about you?"

"I'll go right after you're finished."

Duvall counted the coins and looked at the buxom redhead, imagining how it'd feel to hold her robust naked charms in his arms. Then, bent forward like a hunter, he moved toward her, his eyes glittering brightly, licking his upper lip.

Stone watched him go, and felt as if he'd accomplished something significant. He'd brought the man out of the cave and back into the mainstream of life, reclaiming him for society, transforming him into a productive worker and patron of the erotic arts.

"Whiskey!" he shouted to the bartender.

The bartender poured the glass, and Stone turned toward the back of the saloon, where men tossed chips on gaming tables wreathed in tobacco smoke.

A slim figure loomed up in front of him, wearing a blue shirt and a blue Union Army forage cap with a black visor. The man had black hair on his chest and stopped cold in his tracks when he saw Stone's Confederate cavalry hat.

Both men jerked their hands toward their guns, then froze and glowered at each other. Men in the vicinity got out of their way. The former Yankee soldier was five feet ten, flat-stomached, compactly built, solid in his aspect.

Then they smiled sheepishly at each other, and broke into laughter.

"By God," Stone said, "I don't even know you, and I was ready to shoot your lights out!"

"You don't know how close to the grave you were," the Yankee said. "Let me buy you a drink."

"No, I'll buy you one."

"I insist."

"So do I."

Again they glowered at each other, then burst into laughter again. The Yankee held out his hand. "Name's Calvin Blakemore."

"John Stone, and you've got a lot of guts, walking around Texas in that hat."

Blakemore shrugged. "Mr. Colt has always taken care of me in the past, and he'll take care of me in the future."

"What're you doing out here?"

"That's what I'm trying to figure out. How about you?"

"I'm trying to break into the cattle business."

"Supposed to be a lot of money in it, but men have lost their asses too."

"It's that way with anything. I've just signed on with an outfit leaving for Kansas in about a week, and they're looking for men, if you're interested. They pay thirty dollars a month, plus your chuck, and everybody says the cook is a wizard, although he hates my guts."

"Why's that?"

"I used to own the son of a bitch, and it sticks in his craw."

"I guess you're plannin' to lose some weight, him bein' the cook and all."

"He tries anything with me, I'll hand him his black head on a platter."

The bartender filled their glasses with whiskey, while Stone and Blakemore argued who was going to pay.

The bartender asked, "Why don't you flip a coin?"

Blakemore tossed one behind his back, caught it in his teeth, and dropped it into his open palm. "I pay," he said, dropping some coins on the bar. Then he lifted the glass in his hand and delivered the toast: "Faster horses, younger women, older whiskey, and more money!"

They touched the rims of their glasses, and tossed the whiskey down. Then Blakemore looked at Stone. "You know, you and I might've met during the war, and I would've shot you off yer horse, because I've done that to men who wore hats like your'n, but instead here we are in San Antone, drinking whiskey together, and I heard they got dancing girls."

"And if I saw you in those days," Stone replied, "I'd cut you down, because I've done it before to Yankees in blue hats, but thank God we didn't kill each other, because the bartender told me the dancing girls come out in a few minutes."

The bartender poured two more whiskeys, and Stone felt his head floating in the air above the bar, like a hot-air reconnaissance balloon. Billy Yank and Johnny Reb raised their glasses and gulped the whiskey down.

"I'm tired of the damned war!" Stone said. "Let's talk about anything except the war!"

"They can shove the war up their ass, for all I care," Blakemore replied. "Only damn fools talk about the war, and the more they talk about it, the farther they were from the front. You been upstairs yet? They say it's a hot place."

"After I finish this drink, I'm going."

"You can take the whiskey with you."

"I'm in no hurry."

"I was born in a hurry, and I'm in the mood for a woman. See you down here later, and maybe I'll take that cowboy job, but if I don't see you again, I'm glad I never shot you off'n yer horse." Blakemore drained his glass, winked roguishly, and strolled into the teeming crowd, heading for the wide staircase.

For five years, Stone saved himself for the woman he loved, and now had to adjust to his new freedom. He could do all the things he'd dreamed of, and nothing would stop him.

There was no point keeping his distance from women anymore, never daring to touch those delicious curves, the napes of their necks, those supple legs that wrapped around a man and twisted him into ecstasy.

Now he could do it all. *Marie, wherever you are, you'd better get yours, because from now on I'm getting mine.* Opening his shirt pocket, he took out her picture. She looked at the photographer, a faint smile on her face, and she was a dead ringer for Cassandra Whiteside. "So long, kid," Stone said. "It's been good to know you."

He poised the photograph in his fingers, ready to chuck it

into the filthy spit-encrusted spittoon next to the rail, when something stopped him. He wouldn't want her to do that to his picture, and he had no right to be mad at her, people can't help who they fall in love with. She'd always been straight with him, except for a few episodes here and there, but nobody's perfect, and she deserved better than a spittoon. He returned the photograph to his shirt pocket, buttoned it, and drained his glass.

Sometimes a man can drink for hours, and then take a gulp that will floor him. The last swallow had that effect on Stone, and his head swam with images of Marie, Cassandra, his parents, Yankees in blue coats charging at Sharpsburg. He gripped the bar for support and closed his eyes. *This stuff is killing me.*

He knew if he held on long enough, his mind would come back. Gradually the saloon cleared and he felt strong again. He reached into his pocket for money to buy another drink.

There wasn't much left, and it annoyed him that he was always counting pennies. Insufficient funds forced him to lead a cramped miserable life, and it was getting on his nerves.

"Bartender—where the hell are you!"

The Mexican in the white shirt was working the other end of the bar, and didn't pay any attention to Stone, who felt blind rage coming over him. Nothing turned out right, he'd searched for a ghost, and what did he have to show for it? Not a goddamn thing. His emotions boiled like soup in a pot as the bartender approached. "Señor?"

Stone reached over the bar and grabbed the front of the bartender's shirt. "Let me tell you something. I don't like it when I call a bartender, and he ignores me. Don't let it happen again. Do we understand each other?"

The Mexican's eyes stared into Stone's. "We understand each other, señor."

"Fill this glass with whiskey!"

Something hit Stone like a longhorn steer on a rampage, flinging him through the air. He bounced off a pillar, sprawled onto a table, knocked it over, and landed in a pile of ashtrays, glasses, and playing cards.

Stone climbed to his feet, whirled, and saw a stocky Mexican in a wide white sombrero, tight-fitting brown vaquero pants that flared at the bottoms, and high-topped, well-worn black riding roots.

"Fill your own glass with whiskey, gringo," the Mexican said. "A man does not talk that way to another man."

Stone realized the Mexican was right, and a man doesn't talk to another man like that, but you can't back down from a Mexican in a Texas saloon. He moved his hands over his guns, but didn't feel confident, because he was in the wrong.

"There is no need for any of that, gringo. Apologize to the bartender, and I will forget everything. But if you want to be ridiculous, I will kill you."

Stone spread his legs apart, loosened his fingers, and got ready for the quick-draw that would send one of them to hell, because he was too angry at the world to apologize to a Mexican in a Texas saloon.

A figure moved between them, and it was Luke Duvall, arms outstretched in supplication. "Don Emilio," he said, "have pity on this poor dumb gringo! He was hurt in the war, and his woman has just left him. On top of that, he drinks too much, and he was *un poquito loco* to begin with. He meant no harm— just a lost *caballero* like all the rest of us here."

Don Emilio shrugged. "He cannot be so bad, if he has a friend like you to speak for him. I will forgive him this time. But next time, God will have to forgive him. *Vamanos, muchachos!*"

A crowd of vaqueros gathered around Don Emilio, and they walked toward the swinging doors. They numbered nine men, armed with guns in holsters and knives in belts.

Duvall walked toward Stone. "You're one crazy son of a bitch, but that time I believe you took it about as far as you'll ever take it. That's Don Emilio Maldonado, and he lives in the brush country down by the Nueces, and nobody ever, I repeat *ever*, messes with him."

Stone felt as if a tornado had thrown him into the air, and just had let him down gently. He took a deep breath and pushed his hat back on his head. "Maybe I'd better stop drinking. Hey— wait a minute! You're back! How did it go?"

"There ain't nothin' like a real woman with a real ass, so we're plannin' to git married as soon as we find a preacher man, and we want you to be best man!"

Stone stared at him. "Now let me get this straight. You just spent three years in a cave, and now, your first day back at the rodeo, you're getting married?"

"I know it has a certain ring to it, but that's the way it is."

"When do I meet the bride?"

"Soon as she goes on her break."

"You mean she'll continue working at her profession?"

"Both of us savin' our pennies, we'll have our own herd in two years, but you almost just got yerself killed, whether you realize it or not."

Stone smiled grimly. "He would've done me a favor."

"You sound like me before I went to the cave."

"Since you're leaving the cave, I guess I should move right in before somebody else finds it."

Duvall pointed his finger at him. "I told you when we first met—you'll end up in a cave."

They laughed, wrapped their arms around each other's shoulders, and shuffled toward the bar. In the corner, a man in a striped shirt, with red garters around his biceps, fingered the keyboard of a piano. Stone placed one foot on the brass rail and said in a moderate tone, "Bartender?"

The Mexican man in the white shirt walked toward him. "Señor?"

"Two whiskeys, and I'm sorry if I insulted you, but I got bad news today, and you know how it is when you get bad news."

"I understand, señor. One day my wife told me her mother is coming to live with us, and I throw the table out the window."

The bartender poured the whiskeys, and at that moment Calvin Blakemore appeared beside Stone, and Blakemore's Yankee forage cap was low over his eyes. "Pour one for me too," he said in a deep voice, standing tall and lean, one foot on the rail.

He had a calm, satisfied expression on his face, and so did Duvall. Stone knew it was his turn, and he thought: *What the hell.* He had the money, he had the time, and all he had to do was walk upstairs, pick one out, and cut loose.

He heard a drumroll, and turned toward the far corner of the saloon. A band had set itself up around the piano player, and

the trumpet began to play. Everybody applauded, and one of
the vaqueros shouted, *"Arriba!"*

Every eye in the saloon turned to the top of the staircase,
and standing there were five women in purple and gold tights,
and the one in the middle, with long, straight black hair parted
in the middle, sang, in a German accent:

> "I'm chust a little cowgirl
> alone in the barn
> von't you come undt play vith me?"

Stone stared transfixed. She was nearly six feet tall, supple
as a gazelle, with substantial breast development, and a throaty
smoky voice that said whiskey drunk here.

The dancers descended the stairs while the tall one continued
to sing:

> "I've got my saddle
> and bridle
> but nothing to ride
> von't you come undt play vith me?"

She threw a flower into the audience, and the men cheered.
She and the other dancers waved their fans, casting naughty
glances at the lust-maddened cowboys, whose tongues hung
out of their mouths, like cattle.

Stone watched her with the eyes of a connoisseur of women.
If a man was going to get laid, after five years of nothing,
he should have something like that. The band picked up the
tempo, and the women broke into a dance, moving saucily
among the tables. Stone touched his hands to his guns, to
make sure they still were there, because he expected trouble.

Miraculously no one grabbed the dancers, and the tall one
moved seductively to the bar, singing to each lovesick fool
standing with a drink in his hand, and she blew kisses to them
as she sashayed along.

She came abreast of Stone, and he blew her a kiss back. Calvin
Blakemore snorted beside him. "You never made enough in the
best year of yer life, to pay for a night with that one."

"I think she likes me," Stone replied.

"You and every other man in this shithouse."

Stone watched her arch her shapely back, and then she was swallowed up by the smoke at the rear of the saloon. Stone sighed as he rolled a cigarette and listened to the lilt of her voice:

"I'm chust a little cowgirl
vaiting for the man
who lives in my dreams
vhy don't you come undt play vith me?"

Her voice became fainter, and Stone heard Duvall clear his throat next to him. Stone turned in his direction and saw him standing beside a redhead.

"I want you to meet Miss Eulalie Parker," Duvall said stiffly.

Stone tipped his hat. "Pleased to meet you."

She looked at him boldly, and her expression said: *I know what you think of me, but say it and you'll have this tray of drinks in your face.*

"Your prospective husband has asked me to be the best man at your wedding," Stone said to her. "I find this remarkable, since you two only met an hour ago. I can understand his decision, because you're a lovely woman, and he's been living in a cave for three years, but tell me—why in the hell are you marrying *him*?"

She didn't bat an eyelash. "I been with a lot of men in my day, and they twisted me every which way you can imagine, but I ain't never been twisted the way this here man twisted me, and I ain't lettin' him go. That answer yer question?"

"Let me buy the both of you a drink. Bartender?"

The bartender set up the glasses, as the tall woman reappeared in the main part of the saloon, purring a German tune, and the cowboys gazed at her with lust in their hearts. She could be singing about the price of turnips in Bavaria, for all they knew.

Stone examined her once more from the top of her head to the tips of her toes, and decided she was worthy of him. Why go to bed with your basic frontier whore, when you could go to bed with something like that? Marie had been around five-six, but Stone had always wondered, in the deepest most secret part of his mind, what it'd be like to love a woman built to his proportions, like that German singer with the big diamond pendant hanging from the thick gold chain around her neck.

"What's her name?" Stone asked.

"Veronika," replied Eulalie Parker.

"Veronika what."

"Just Veronika."

During the long years he'd searched for Marie, he'd tried not to see other women, so he wouldn't fall in love with one of them, but now the veil had been torn away, and he found himself staring at one of the most voluptuous women he'd ever seen, begging him to play with her.

He stood in the smoky dimness of the saloon, a cigarette dangling out of the corner of his mouth, and his hat perched on the back of his head. He was surrounded by a variety of sombreros, stovepipe hats, modified derbies, and cowboy hats of all types. Every eye was on Veronika as she slipped among them, patting their heads and pinching their noses, driving them wild.

Yesterday the gods had their big laugh when they told him Marie wasn't Cassandra, and today, so he wouldn't become complacent, they threw in Marie's replacement, the woman who appeared to be looking directly at him just then, singing her strange Bavarian love song.

Shamelessly he undressed her with his eyes, and Marie couldn't hold him back any longer. Stone marveled at Veronika's long legs, those abundant breasts, but most of all her bewitching eyes and sinuous mouth. She looked like a Nordic Amazon Queen, and he thought she was just what he needed.

She came to the end of her song, and the audience burst into boisterous applause, as only a frontier audience can. Somebody threw a twenty-dollar gold coin at Veronika's feet, she picked it up deftly; a cowboy fired his gun into the rafters. The crowd surged toward the dancers, and the women blew kisses, then ran daintily up the stairs and disappeared into the murky depths of the second-floor whorehouse.

Stone felt touched by a magic wand. He was coming to life again, the cloud that had been over his head was passing, everything would be all right from now on, he was free to forge his destiny, and with that incredible woman at his side, there'd be nothing he couldn't accomplish. He looked up at the second floor.

Blakemore dug his elbow into Stone's ribs. "Forget about it. She's not for the likes of you, Johnny Reb. If you want to git into her laundry, you got to be more than just another saddle tramp."

Stone turned to him. "Now you listen to me, you damned blue belly. I may not look like much now, but I was an officer and a gentleman once, and I've had a first-class education. You may find it hard to believe, but not every woman is looking for whatever a man has in his pocket. Some women fall in love with a man's spirit."

Blakemore looked at Stone, and saw a ragged vagabond with a mad gleam in his eyes. He slapped Stone on the shoulder. "Johnny Reb," he said, "you remind me of the flea who wanted to marry the elephant. But I'm a sportin' man, as I'm sure you are. I'll bet you five dollars, cash on the barrelhead, that you'll never get into the bed of that high-priced drink of water what was just singin' out here."

"You're on!" Stone said.

Stone fished five dollars out of his pocket, and Blakemore pulled the same amount out of his. Solemnly, they gave the money to Duvall.

"How'll I know whether or not you do it?" Blakemore asked Stone.

"You'll have to take my word for it, but you needn't worry, my word is good. I used to be an officer and a gentleman."

"And I used to be the king of San Francisco. I think I just made a bad bet."

"You did, but not for the reason you think. Bartender, may I please have another glass of whiskey?"

Stone's head was spinning, and he coughed from the volume of cigarette and cigar smoke around him; the roulette wheel couldn't be seen from the bar anymore. Stone wanted to go someplace, but didn't know where, and didn't realize he was just trying to escape the pain of loneliness now that Marie was gone.

The bartender poured the whiskey, and Stone drank half of it down, then rolled another cigarette. Somehow he'd have to get into her room, and he'd plan it like a military expedition, with a diversion, then the main attack. "Hold 'em by the nose, and kick 'em in the pants" is what Jeb Stuart used to say.

If he just walked upstairs and asked for her, they'd throw him out a window. How could he push through enemy resistance? A waitress walked by, carrying a tray, and he got an idea. When the bartender came into his vicinity, he leaned forward and whispered into his ear.

Blakemore nudged Stone again. "Why don't you admit you're just afraid? You ain't kiddin' me, Johnny Reb. It'd be easy for you to go upstairs and screw one of 'em, but instead you have to go for somethin' impossible, so you'll fail. What's the matter, Johnny Reb? Can't git it up?"

Stone looked coldly at him. "I ought to kill you, but I've wasted enough good lead on Yankees already. If I go upstairs and pay a whore five dollars, it'll only be a quick professional roll on the mattress, and then your time's up, and the next man walks in. A whore will do it with anybody who puts his money down, and if you paid her to screw a donkey, she'd do it. Billy Yank, I need something a bit more satisfying than that. I need to feel *privileged* in some way. Do you think you can catch a glimmer of what I'm saying?"

Blakemore laughed out of the corner of his mouth. "Son of a bitch is lookin' for true love at the Last Chance Saloon. I'd better roll up my pants,'cause the shit's gittin' deep in here."

The bartender set down a tray with a small bottle of brandy, pot of coffee, cups, saucers, and a white dish towel. Stone reached into his pocket for the money, counted it, and was nearly tapped out. He passed his Confederate cavalry officer's hat to the bartender and said, "Hold this for me." Then he smoothed down his hair, straightened his shirt, took a deep breath, picked up the tray, and folded the dish rag over his arm.

He marched toward the stairs, and they watched him ascend to the second floor. Blakemore turned to Duvall and said, "I'll bet somebody shoots him."

"A miracle he got this far," Duvall replied. He reached for Stone's glass of whiskey and poured the contents into his own empty glass.

Stone walked down the corridor, and a door opened in front of him. A whore and her customer stepped out, and Stone said to her, in his most precise enunciation, because he knew he was loaded: "Could you please tell me where I might find Veronika's room?"

"Down the hall on the other end."

Stone walked in the direction indicated, the bottle of brandy dancing on the tray, and he wondered how real waiters carried their trays so effortlessly. He came to the end of the corridor, and saw a sign that said ENTERTAINMENT. He knocked on the door, it was opened by two men wearing range clothes and hostile suspicion.

"I have something for Veronika," Stone said.

"I'll take it," one of them replied.

"I'll deliver it myself, if you don't mind."

"Gimme the goddamned tray."

"Can't do it. Now if you'll just let me through, I'll . . ."

The one in the red shirt punched him in the stomach, Stone doubled over and dropped the tray; it went crashing toward the floor. The other, in a plaid shirt, hit him with an uppercut, straightening and sending him flying out of the room. Stone landed in the corridor, the taste of blood in his mouth.

"Vhat is going on here?" asked a female voice.

Stone, covered with brandy and hot coffee, looked up and saw Veronika standing like a tall raven-tressed valkyrie in the doorway.

"He was tryin' to break into yer suite, ma'am."

"I wasn't trying to break in," Stone replied, picking himself up off the floor. "I just wanted to talk with you about something important."

She examined his husky shoulders, prominent pectorals, and bulging biceps. "Well," she said with a toss of her head, "everybody else has been annoying me tonight, so vhy not you?"

"I wanted to tell you something that could change your life."

She made a wry smile. "Another lunatic, but I haf alvays had a veakness for lunatics. You may come in for a few minutes, undt tell me how to change my life, because it has become clear to me lately, to judge by my surroundings, that I must be doing something wrong."

Stone followed her like a hound dog who'd picked up the

scent of his prey, passing the two men who looked at him as if he'd just crawled out from underneath a pile of buffalo shit.

She entered a room furnished with a dressing table, a few chairs, and a sofa in front of the window through which shone the light of the sun setting behind mountains in the distance.

She sat at the dressing table, bent forward, and looked at herself in the mirror, pursing her lips, and Stone wanted to rip her clothes off.

"What is this important information?" she asked, brushing cosmetics onto her cheek.

"Let's go to bed, and I'll show you."

She looked at him with new concern. "You are not dangerous, are you?"

"Not at all."

"You should not say things like that to a voman, as if ve are toys to be played vith undt thrown away."

"I'd never throw you away."

She laughed darkly. "That is vhat they all say."

"Listen to me," he said earnestly. "It's rare when two people meet who are so completely matched as the both of us. There aren't many like us left."

She couldn't suppress a smile. "There are millions like you everywhere I go, men who promise to love me forever, then ends the night undt comes the dawn, I look beside me undt they are gone." She gazed at him tenderly. "I know you belief vhat you are saying, but you are lying, to me undt to yourself. My advice to you is haf another drink, undt enjoy the next show. It starts in fifteen minutes, undt I haf to get ready, so if you vill excuse me . . ."

Stone was deflated by the realization that she was right, he had nothing special to offer, not even the price of a hotel room, but he arose and moved toward her.

"Vhere do you think you are going?" she asked, still looking at her face in the mirror.

He touched his hand to her silky hair, then dropped to one knee.

"Stop it," she said.

"I can't."

She punched him in the solar plexus, and the wind went out of him. He dropped to the floor, hugging his chest, gasping.

"I told you," she said with Teutonic crispness, "that I haf to get ready for the next show, but if you come to my hotel later, perhaps ve can haf a drink. I am at the Barlowe House, room three twenty-one, around two in the morning?"

"Could I have a little kiss now, to keep me going?"

"That vill disturb my cosmetics. *Auf wiedersehen, schatzchen.*"

She returned to her cosmetics, as if he weren't there. He opened the door and stepped into the next room. The two bodyguards sat on opposite sides of a table, playing dominoes, and they looked up at him as he passed. He felt tense and crazy, and remembered them beating him in the corridor, for no reason at all. In a sudden impulsive move, he kicked the legs out from one of the chairs, and the bodyguard in the red shirt was dumped to the floor, while the one in the plaid shirt went for his six-gun, but Stone beat him to the draw.

The man's hand froze on the elkhorn grip of his gun, while the one on the floor raised himself to his feet. Veronika's door opened, and she stood backlit by the lamps at her dressing table. "*Schatzchen,* please do not make trouble. Put away your guns undt go now, like a good boy, all right?"

Stone holstered his guns and looked at the bodyguards. "Hope to see you galoots some other time."

"So do we, varmint," said the one in the red shirt.

Stone holstered his guns and walked to the door, stepping into the hall. He wanted whiskey, but first he'd take a walk and clear his head. He stepped onto a small balcony atop a flight of steps that led to the backyard of the hotel, and climbed down, the night breeze cool and pleasant through his hair.

He walked down a dark alley and came to the main street of San Antone. Lamps glowed through the windows of saloons and billiard parlors. Horses were hitched to the rails, and he remembered Tomahawk. He didn't have money left for a stable and whiskey both, so it looked as though the poor animal was going to spend his night in the street, but it wouldn't be the first time, and wouldn't be the last.

Stone noticed a candle in a window, and the sign said:

YOUR FORTUNE TOLD
25 cents

He looked through the window into a small room where an old crone wearing gold earrings and a red silk bandanna on her head sat at a table, looking at him with an amused smile, and then she beckoned to him, her lips forming the words: "Come in, cowboy—I am not going to hurt you."

He hesitated, because he didn't like incense and hocus-pocus. He was about to turn away, when the Gypsy woman came to the door. She wore several skirts, one over the other, and a blouse cut low over her wrinkled shoulders and withered breasts. She stood in the doorway, crossing her arms, looking haughtily at him, and her skin was olive, gleaming in the moonlight.

"Tell your future, cowboy?" she asked in a throaty voice.

"I'm not sure I want to know what it is," he replied.

"You were a soldier once, no?"

"How can you tell?"

"No magic would be required to see that. It is in the way you stand. Ready to jump on your horse and kill somebody, eh, cowboy?"

"A man's got to stay ready."

"The best way to be ready is to know what is coming. That is what I, Madam Lazonga, can do for you. I will tell your future, your past, and answer five questions of your choice, for only twenty-five cents. Never in your life will you find a bargain like this, cowboy, never."

Stone puffed his cigarette and blew smoke rings in the air as he regarded her. "You flimflamming like everybody else?"

"It will only cost twenty-five cents, and at the very least, I will amuse you for a while. That is not so much money, is it? Why, one would think I was asking for your first-born child, the way you are acting!"

It wasn't much money, and maybe she did know something. "All right," he said, "but make it good."

"That part is up to you, but I'll give you a cup of tea, at no extra charge."

He followed her into a room whose walls were covered with beads and fringed curtains. It was furnished with a round table and two chairs, and in the middle of the table sat a crystal ball on a purple velvet cushion, with a lit candle on each side.

"Sit down," she said. "Relax and smoke your cigarette. I will be back with the tea."

He bent forward and peered into the crystal ball, colored lights sparkling and gleaming within its crystal depths. *What am I doing here?*

She returned, carrying a pot with two cups and saucers. "Drink," she said. "Relax. Tell me who you are, so I might know you better."

"I'm a drifter, and I just got a job today as a cowboy for the Triangle Spur."

"Once you were wealthy, yes?"

"How did you know?"

"I don't know how I know. I just know. You have had terrible disappointments in your life, I see that too. And women have loved you, but that would be obvious even to a woman who was not a Gypsy, yet I, with my Gypsy eyes, can see far deeper than that. I see the friends who died on the battlefield, and I see the bullet that struck you on your body just beneath your ribs, on the left side, and nearly killed you. Yes, I see lots of things. Give me your hand, please."

How could she know about that old battle scar?

"I asked for your hand, cowboy."

He gave it to her, she kneaded it with her strong fingers garnished with baubled rings, then flattened it, brought the candle closer, and gazed at the wrinkles and creases. "Oh," she said, as if she'd been taken by surprise.

"What is it?"

She let go of his hand. "To tell you the truth, palmistry is not really my specialty. Drink your tea, and we will work better with the crystal ball."

"You saw something in my hand, and I'd like to know what it was."

"How can you believe this foolishness? I am only a poor old Gypsy, and I have gyped you out of twenty-five cents. Call the sheriff if you like, but I think it would be best if you leave now."

"Madam Lazonga," he said, "we made a deal, and now you're backing out. If you don't hold up your end"—he took out a match—"I'll burn this building to the ground, and if you look into my eyes, you can see I'm crazy enough to do it."

She gazed into his eyes, her brow furrowed. "It will be a long and difficult reading."

"I'll pay for your time."

"Cross my palm with silver."

Stone gave her another quarter.

"Again."

He dropped more coins onto her wrinkled hand, and she dropped them between her breasts. Then she took his hand. "What do you want to know first—the future, the past, or prospects for love?"

"I want to know what you just saw in my hand, and don't ask me to cross your palm with silver again, because I'm flat broke."

"This is your life line," she said, pointing a long red fingernail. "Are you sure you want to know?"

"It's like you said before: it's best to know so you can be prepared."

"You cannot be prepared for death, cowboy. When it comes, it comes like an eagle out of the night, grasping you suddenly and carrying you away."

"What does it say?"

"It says . . . you are going . . . to die young."

Stone sat silently as the Gypsy's curse sank into him. Was she a swindler, or did she know what she was talking about?

"Do not worry," she said. "There is nothing you can do about it, and who knows, maybe you are right and I am only a swindler. Shall I go on?"

"When will I die?"

"Your palm does not carry a date. It only says you will die when you are young."

"What's young?"

She shrugged. "What's young to you? It's your palm, not mine. How old would you be, if you didn't know how old you were?"

"What else do you see?"

She held his palm in her cold bony fingers and brought her slanted rheumy eyes closer. "You will love well, but not wisely. You will travel far. Someday you will have great wealth. You will suffer much." She took a deep breath, as if she'd just undergone a great exertion, and leaned back in her chair. "You haven't touched your tea."

He raised the cup and sipped the hot liquid, which tickled as it rolled over his tongue. It had a citrus flavor, and he gulped it down.

The crystal ball radiated pulsations of light that reflected in Madam Lazonga's eyes. "The spirits are calling me," she intoned mysteriously, bending over the gleaming orb. "I see a woman with golden hair, who loves you very much."

"Where is she?" Stone asked.

"In the setting sun. And I see another woman, who is dead. She is your mother, and she too loves you very much. How lucky you are, to be loved like this."

"The woman with the golden hair—I'd like to know more about her."

"You are going on a long journey, and you will have many difficulties, but it is your destiny, and you cannot avoid it. I see you afterward in a big city, much bigger than this, and the woman with the golden hair is there with you."

Stone stared at her. "Are you sure?"

She undulated her hands before the crystal ball and brought her eyes closer to it. "I see a black master crossing your path. Beware of him, but one day he will cheat the Gypsy's curse. And last of all I see an old friend who will lead you on a second journey to a far-off land."

She paused and blinked. A naked little girl with gold earrings waddled into the room, sucking her thumb. "I want to go to bed, Granma. When you tuck me in?"

Madam Lazonga said something in a strange foreign language to the child, then turned to Stone. "That is all, cowboy. You want to know more, you come back some other time."

"Tell me more about the woman with golden hair?"

"You will see her someday, according to the crystal ball. There is nothing to worry about. Good night."

She leaned forward and blew out the candles, plunging the room into darkness.

4

STUMBLING BACK TO the Last Chance Saloon, Stone thought about the Gypsy's curse, and could swear there was something strange in the tea she'd given him.

He saw balloons and confetti, but there was no parade. His burnished spurs jangled, but he didn't feel his boots touch the ground. He floated through the doors of the Last Chance Saloon, and saw the usual bunch of killers, thieves, pickpockets, gamblers, and saints dumped into one combination saloon, casino, and whorehouse.

Stone made his way to the bar, his eyes half-closed, and all he wanted was another glass of whiskey. He only had a few coins left in his jeans, but he had a horse and a job, so he stepped to the bar, placed one foot on the rail, and said, "Bartender!"

A different bartender was on duty, a heavyset, middle-aged American wearing a dirty apron. "Whiskey?"

Stone nodded, and the bartender poured. Stone thought about the top floor of the Barlowe House at two in the morning, and the delights that awaited him there. Then he remembered Marie, and took out her picture. "It was good while it lasted," he said to her, "but all good things come to an end." Again he contemplated throwing it into the nearest spittoon, and again dropped it back into his shirt pocket.

He lit a cigarette, sipped whiskey, and it was like a hundred other nights in a hundred other saloons. The lamps made a sheen on his cheeks, and his hair was mussed. He couldn't remember what happened to his old Confederate cavalry hat, and there was something important he had to do, but he couldn't remember what.

"Señor, can I buy you a drink?"

Stone turned and saw Don Emilio Maldonado standing next to him, his wide sombrero low over his eye.

"I never turn down a free drink," Stone said.

"Nor do I." Don Emilio called the bartender, who instantly stopped what he was doing and came running toward them over the slats behind the bar.

"Double whiskeys, for my friend and me."

The bartender poured the brew, and Don Emilio looked up at Stone, a faint smile on his face. "I have heard you apologized for your rude behavior to the other bartender, and it takes a real *hombre* to do that. If you are ever down in the brush country, ask for me, and I will offer you my hospitality, as one *caballero* to another, yes?"

"Like I said, I never turn down a free drink."

"What is your name?"

"John Stone."

"*Juan Piedra*. That is what it would be in Spanish. What are you doing in San Antonio?"

"Not a goddamn thing."

"Need a job?"

"I've got a job."

"If you ever come to the brush country, you can work for me. It is a hard life, but an *hombre* can feel like an *hombre*. We will drink mescal, and I will tell you of the women I've loved, and the men I've killed, and you will tell me of the women you've loved, and the men you've killed." Don Emilio raised his glass, drained it, and slammed it down on the bar. *"Hasta luego, gringo."*

Don Emilio walked toward two tables surrounded by Mexican vaqueros drinking, laughing, and playing cards.

Stone looked into his fresh glass of whiskey and thought: *One moment a man's going to blow you away, and the next moment he buys you a whiskey.* He raised the glass carefully, slurped off an inch, then sucked air between his clenched teeth and placed the glass on the bar again.

He was hungry, and didn't have the price of a meal. Maybe he should've borrowed a few dollars from Don Emilio, while that *hombre* was in a good mood. Then suddenly he realized what he was supposed to do. He was supposed to feed and water Tomahawk. The poor animal was probably starving to death, while he was drinking whiskey, chasing dancing girls, and getting into trouble.

Stone's head did another pirouette, he leaned his elbows on the bar. It was getting late, and he thought he'd just go off with Tomahawk to a grassy watering spot, and fall asleep with all the other prairie dogs.

He lifted the glass to his lips again, and somebody behind him said, "There he is!"

Stone turned around and saw the two bodyguards from the Barlowe House. He looked at them, and his demons urged him on. They'd jumped him in the hallway, punched him around, and prevented him from being alone with the fair Veronika.

"We been lookin' fer you," said red shirt.

"I haven't been hiding," Stone replied.

The two bodyguards looked at each other, turned down the corners of their mouths, and charged.

Stone lunged when they came close, throwing a straight right through the smoke at the nose of plaid shirt, and plaid shirt raised his arms to block the punch, while red shirt slammed Stone in the kidney with a left hook.

It felt like a knife, but Stone was in the middle of a fight and had to keep on until he dropped. Red shirt raised his fist for a shot at Stone's face, but Stone danced to the side, distancing himself from the punch, and cut loose with a vicious left jab to the mouth of plaid shirt, connecting, stopping him cold, but meanwhile red shirt rushed forward, diving toward Stone, hoping to tackle and bring him down.

Stone timed him coming in and kicked him in the face, and red shirt went flying backward, crashing into a table. Meanwhile, plaid shirt recovered from the punch in the mouth, and hurled a right cross toward Stone's head, but Stone leaned to the side, and the punch whistled harmlessly by his ear.

Stone stepped forward, got inside, and hooked plaid shirt's body with a left, right, and left, then went upstairs and landed a blow that made plaid shirt's head snap to the side. Plaid shirt fell on his back, just as red shirt arose from the floor. He stood and faced Stone, both men breathing through open mouths.

Stone was afraid red shirt didn't want to fight anymore, and that wasn't what Stone wanted. The wildness and madness were on him now, his life was a mess, nothing he did turned out right, he didn't have long to live, and he wanted to kick the shit out of somebody.

The man in the red shirt didn't disappoint him. A bottle sat on a nearby table, and he snatched it, backhanding it against the edge of the table, and glass and whiskey flew in all directions. He held the bottle's jagged edge in the air and took a step forward.

"Are you sure that's the way you want it?" Stone asked.

Red shirt got lower and advanced toward Stone, light from the lamps glinting off the cruel points of the broken bottle, and that was his answer. Stone bent over and pulled his knife out of his boot. It had a ten-inch blade, and was a gift from an Apache named Lobo, one of the best knife fighters Stone had ever seen.

Stone held the knife blade up, waved it back and forth like a head of a cobra, and said, "Come on!"

Red shirt's mouth was set in a grim line, while drinkers, gamblers, and whores stepped back out of the way. The Last Chance Saloon had become silent as a church during the meditation hour. Meanwhile, plaid shirt lifted himself from the floor and watched, his right hand near his gun. Stone saw the crowd gather around them, and knew everybody wanted to see blood. Among them he saw the big sombreros of Don Emilio Maldonado and his vaqueros, but nobody intervened.

Stone's old soldierly fighting spirit came back, and he held the knife tightly in his fist, stepping toward the man in the red shirt, knowing one of them was going to die.

They circled each other in front of the bar, every eye on them, and the gamblers took bets, with the odds five to three in favor of Stone's opponent, because everybody knew him, a local gun for hire, whereas Stone was just another saddle tramp, and he looked bleary-eyed, half in the bag.

Red shirt's teeth were yellowed by tobacco, and he made a twisted smile as he crouched lower, beckoning with his left hand.

"Whatcha waitin' fer, cowboy?" he asked. "Let's do it."

Stone feinted a thrust at red shirt's gut, and red shirt lowered his defense, which was just what Stone wanted. Stone raised his knife and slashed out at red shirt's face, but red shirt raised his bottle in the nick of time, there was a clash, and steel cut through glass, spraying shards into the air.

Both combatants took a quick step backward, but there was no damage except the broken bottle demolished in red shirt's hand.

Red shirt dropped the broken bottle, reached behind him, and yanked a knife out of its scabbard attached to his belt. It was a Tennessee toothpick, with a slim, double-sided eight-inch blade, razor-sharp on both sides, as deadly a weapon as a man could carry.

They circled each other again, crouching low, holding their knives in front of them, blades up, then switched directions and circled the other way. Stone measured his opponent, looking for an opening, he only needed that inch that could spell the difference between another glass of whiskey or eternity in a dank, cold grave.

He saw it and went in for the kill, streaking the point of his blade toward his opponent's heart, but red shirt chopped down with the blade of his Tennessee toothpick and sliced open Stone's forearm.

Stone jumped back quickly, his arm on fire, and readied himself for the follow-up charge. He didn't have to wait long. With a victorious shout, red shirt leapt forward, back-slashing at Stone's face, but Stone ducked under the blow and jabbed his knife upward into red shirt's soft underbelly.

There was no resistance, and Stone's ten inches of Apache steel went in all the way to the hilt. The man in the red shirt gasped, and blood welled out of his mouth. He looked at Stone quizzically, as if he suddenly discovered that the world was a different place from what he'd thought, and then his knees buckled and he dropped to the floor at Stone's feet.

Stone looked down at him for a moment, and knew he'd never get up again. Then he turned toward the man in the plaid shirt, whose hand still hovered above his six-gun.

"Well?" Stone asked, holding the bloody Apache knife in his right hand, while his left hand moved closer to the Colt in the holster on that side.

Plaid shirt hesitated. "I'm willin' to walk away if you are," he said.

"I got no place to walk," Stone replied, his fingers an inch above the handle of his Colt.

"Too bad for you," plaid shirt said.

Plaid shirt shuffled away, his spurs jangling with every step, and Stone could drill him easily, but southern gentlemen didn't shoot people in the back.

Stone turned toward the bar, reached for his glass of whiskey, and took a swig. Behind him was a commotion, as men carried the dead body outside. He wrapped his bandanna around his cut forearm, and then something behind the bar caught his eye: his old Confederate cavalry hat hanging near a row of whiskey bottles beneath the wide mirror.

"Bartender—could you pass me my hat, please?"

The bartender handed it to him and said, "You look like you could use a drink on the house."

Stone looked at himself in the mirror as he placed his old Confederate cavalry officer's hat on his head, slanting it low over his eyes. For a moment he could see himself in Wade Hampton's headquarters with all the other troop commanders, receiving the order of battle for tomorrow morning, but then he saw cowboy hats and sombreros all around him, and knew he was just another drunk, hoping someone would stand him the next round. Something in back of his mind told him he had a task to perform, and he was trying to figure out what it was when someone touched him on the shoulder.

Stone turned and saw a young preacher with a pimply face and a button nose looking at him sternly. "You just killed a man, and I tell you solemnly that your soul will roast in hell until the end of time, unless you pray to the Lord God for forgiveness! You should've turned the other cheek!"

"If I turned the other cheek, he would've shot me in the back."

The preacher stared at him. "The blood on your hands can be washed away, but the stain in your heart will always be there unless you repent."

Stone felt the whiskey heat his blood. He looked at the black-suited preacher man and saw a buzzard staring back at him. "Move on, preacher man. I got no time for you."

The preacher stared back into Stone's ice-blue eyes. "It's not too late to repent, for the Lord is good, His ways are just, and His mercy is everlasting. You must turn from killing, drinking, and whoring, and follow the path of the Lord, or you'll burn forever in the flames of hell."

Stone saw an immense conflagration envelop him. The flames licked his body for a few moments, and he felt the furnace, then they disappeared, and Stone stood at the bar in the Last Chance Saloon. The preacher pointed his finger at Stone's face.

"You know what I say is true," he said. "You'll find my church on Elm Street, and my name is Brother Ezra. I will pray with you whenever you want, day or night, at your convenience."

Brother Ezra walked away, and Stone turned back to his whiskey. Brother Ezra had evoked his religious training in that small white church back in South Carolina, where it had been drummed into his head every Sunday that a man should do justice, honor truth, and walk humbly with his God.

He'd been flippant with the preacher, but believed everything the preacher had told him: killing was wicked, blasphemy worse, and whiskey could kill a man.

He knew he should get down on his knees and pray to the Lord God for forgiveness, and then go out and change his ways, but he'd been educated in the profession of arms, and then hurled into a war where it had been his sworn duty to kill as many Yankees as possible.

Now everything was mixed up in his mind, and Marie was gone forever, the Gypsy said he hadn't long to live, and he had nothing to live for anyway, but there was something he had to do, and couldn't remember what it was.

Somebody smacked him so hard on the shoulder he nearly lost his balance. Hanging on to the bar for support, he saw Calvin Blakemore and Luke Duvall, both smoking big cigars and wearing wide smiles. They appeared to be at the heights of drunken jubilation, and Duvall's shirt pocket sprouted a handful of cigars.

"We been lookin' all over for you," Blakemore said. "Where you been?"

"Where'd you steal the cigars?"

Blakemore aimed his thumb at Duvall. "This crimp, who's been livin' in a cave for three years, has won eighty dollars at monte!"

Both of them were drunk, and Duvall dug his hand into his pocket, pulled out a handful of coins, and dropped them onto the bar. "Drink up!" he hollered.

"Do you think you could lend me the price of a meal?" Stone asked hopefully.

"I'm hungry too," Duvall roared. "Let's git somethin' ter *eat*!"

"Best grit in town is at Pancho's," Blakemore said, grinning crazily, "and they give you the most!"

"What're we waiting for?" Duvall roared. He grabbed Stone by his red bandanna and pulled him toward the swinging doors.

Stone tripped, regained his footing, and followed Duvall and Blakemore outside to the street, where a group of men sat on their horses, passing a bottle around. The moonlight and street lamps shone on them, as Stone, Blakemore, and Duvall placed their arms around each other's shoulders and marched down the sidewalk, heading toward Pancho's singing at the tops of their lungs:

> "I'm the man
> who broke the bank
> in San Antonio!"

Cassandra sat in her office, trying to figure out what happened to ten thousand dollars. She'd detected the discrepancy late that afternoon, and had been examining the maze of her and her husband's financial dealings ever since, but the money hadn't turned up.

If it was gone, the Triangle Spur was in worse trouble than she'd thought. Drafts had been written against the money, and creditors wouldn't be paid. They'd show up soon demanding money, and Texans usually settled their difficulties with guns.

She wasn't an accountant, and might've put a sum into the wrong column, although she'd been looking for hours and hadn't found it yet.

Her head hurt, her vision blurred, and she felt her bones turning to jelly. It was time to go to bed, and tomorrow she'd find the discrepancy, if that's what it was. She arose, blew out the lamp, and walked soundlessly down the hall to the master bedroom, undressed in the moon shadows, and gazed down at the master bed, where her husband lay on his side, snoring softly.

His truss hung from the bedpost, because he'd suffered that injury too in the war, and he had a paunch, but to Cassandra he still looked like the noble Galahad in the portrait downstairs, hand resting on his sword.

She dropped a flimsy nightgown over her curvaceous body and crawled into bed with him, snuggling against the sweet aroma that emanated from his body, because he bathed daily and administered a variety of lotions and unguents to his skin.

Somehow, for some strange reason, she thought of John Stone. She'd seen him ride out earlier, and he was probably in a whorehouse like all the rest of the men, except her husband, whose standards were too high. Poor John Stone had a dream that exploded in his face. Such a man was capable of anything.

She found herself worrying about him, because he was like a little boy whose puppy just died, and now that she thought of it, Stone had been boyish in many ways, such as his twinkling mischievous eyes, and the play in the corner of his mouth when her husband had been holding forth about the war. She guessed that Stone had been a real terror when he was young.

He reminded her of the wounded soldiers in the New Orleans hospital where she'd visited her cousin Frank. They all had the same haunted look, as if they couldn't assimilate all they'd seen.

So sad, she thought, drifting off into slumber.

The rough-hewn tables groaned under the weight of platters covered with enchiladas, burritos, tortillas, mountains of refried beans, towers of broiled chorizo sausages, the head of a goat, the leg of a pig, the braised testicles of a bull, a variety of chicken parts, garlands of black blood sausage, and lots of bottles.

Stone, Blakemore, and Duvall sat at a table in a corner, and they were the only gringos in a hole in the wall filled to brimming with Mexican men and women eating, laughing, smoking, and most of all drinking.

Blakemore's mouth was full of food as he grabbed a pitcher of cold beer off the tray of a passing Mexican waitress and filled his glass to the brim, the white foam spilling down the sides of the glass onto a table carved with initials and expressions in Spanish. Then he turned to John Stone. "You look like somebody killed your best friend, Johnny Reb. What's on yer mind?"

"Nothing that would interest a damn Yankee."

"Why is it, Johnny Reb, that you can't answer a simple goddamn question—what's eating you?"

Luke Duvall interjected, "He was like that when he fust came to the cave. Din't want to volunteer no information, as if somebody gives a rat's ass about his life, and what he done, and what bothers him."

Stone raised his finger drunkenly in the air, as six inches behind him a Mexican vaquero kissed his girlfriend on the mouth, and she dug her bloodred fingernails into his back. "I was talking to a Gypsy woman," Stone said, "and she told me I was going to die young, and somehow, I don't know exactly why, it bothers me, do you know what I mean?"

Blakemore said, "Madam Lazonga! She told me the same damn thing, after I crossed her palm with silver a few times. That the way it went with you?"

"She saw something, and I had to pay extra to find out what."

"Whether you're a Yankee or a rebel," Blakemore said, "that woman will cheat you anyways."

Duvall replied, "We ought to teach her a lesson. Why don't I go see her, and when she tells me the same story, you two walk in. We'll see how she talks her way out of it."

Stone smiled. "I like the ring of that."

"So do I," said Blakemore, "but first I want a few more of these burritos, and we ain't even *seen* what they got for dessert yet, so don't rush a man while he's stuffin' his face, boys,'cause it ain't healthy."

Stone thought of how gullible he'd been. The Gypsy cheated him, but that's why they called them Gypsies, and he would've worried about dying young for the rest of his life.

Somebody touched his shoulder, and Stone turned to Pancho, portly and sweaty, wearing a dirty apron. "Don Emilio requests that you have a drink with him at his table, señor."

"Be right back," Stone said to Blakemore and Duvall.

Stone threaded past the crowded tables, and saw Don Emilio sitting in the corner with a young Mexican woman on his lap. Don Emilio was hatless, one arm was wrapped around his girl, and she was sticking her tongue into his ear.

Don Emilio held a black cigarillo in his free hand, and beckoned to the empty chair. Stone sat on it, and in the middle of the table was a bottle of clear liquid with something white floating inside. Stone brought his eyes closer to the bottle, and saw that it was a white maggot.

"Have you ever drunk mescal, gringo?"

"Don't believe so."

"Help yourself."

Stone looked at the worm. "I don't think so."

Don Emilio's face clouded. "Why not?"

"What's that worm doing in there?"

"That worm has et up all the poison, and it kill him. I have drunk, Francesca here has drunk, and I am inviting you to drink with us."

"I never turn down free booze," Stone said.

He filled up a glass, raised it to his lips, and said to himself: *I've got to show him what a gringo is made of*—so he swallowed the entire contents of the glass in five steady gulps.

He placed the glass on the table and waited for the kick, as his eyes glazed over. But the kick didn't come, only a warm glow from deep in his belly. "This stuff isn't bad," he said.

"The worm gives it that special taste," Don Emilio replied, and Francesca still had her tongue in his ear.

Stone filled another glass and drank an inch off the top. He'd heard about mescal, but this was the first time he'd tried it.

"I wanted to tell you," Don Emilio said, "that I saw your fight earlier. Where did you learn to use a knife like that?"

"Was in Arizona, and watched Apaches."

"Why were you in Arizona?"

"Looking for a woman, but not anymore."

"You were in love with her?"

"Still am."

"Then you'll never stop looking for her, though you might try."

Francesca withdrew her tongue from his ear. "Do you love me, Don Emilio?" she asked.

"You know I do, *mi mariposa blanca.*"

"Yes," she said, raising one eyebrow, "and the moment you find somebody else who catches your eye, you will love her too."

Don Emilio laughed, his straight white teeth flashing in the light of candles. "I love beautiful flowers, *chiquita*, I do not lie to you."

"I do not know why I stay with you," she said with a pout. "You are so bad."

She snuggled against him, and he said to Stone sadly, "Everything I have ever done in my life, I have done for women, so they would love me, and all they do is tell me I am bad."

Stone looked at him, and it appeared as if Don Emilio's skin was tinged with gold. Red and blue lights flickered behind Don Emilio's head, and Stone felt mildly euphoric. He wanted to laugh, run, sing, anything.

"Why not work for me, gringo?" Don Emilio said. "I am driving my herd to Kansas soon, and I think it would be better for my health if I had some gringo cowboys with me, to smooth over possible, shall we say, *problemas*, because I know what you gringos think of Mexicans. You call us *greasers*, I believe."

"And you call us *gringos*, I believe. Your people and mine fought a war once over these very matters, but I've had too much to drink, and I don't feel like fighting just now, and moreover . . ."

Stone wanted to say something additional, but his mind blanked out. He sat on the chair, eyes half-closed, a crooked smile on his face, or maybe it was a frown.

Don Emilio looked at him with an expression of pity and mild concern. "You will probably not live long, gringo, at the rate you are going. I almost killed you, another man almost killed you, and the night is still young. Why not climb on your horse and go home?"

Stone leaned forward and looked him in the eye. "Because I have a date at two o'clock with a beautiful woman. Do you know the time?"

Don Emilio pulled out a gold watch large as a turnip, carved with ornate designs. "A few minutes after one. I hope she is not far."

"Up the street."

"I would not stop off in any more saloons, if I were you."

"I can take care of myself, Don Emilio. I always have, and I always will."

"You are beginning to think you are invincible, and that is the first step toward your casket. I look at you and see a crazy gringo. You are capable of many things tonight, and I hope love is one of them."

Francesca looked at Stone, through hooded eyes. "This gringo is not bad-looking. I know just the girl for him."

Don Emilio laughed. "This Francesca here, she is Cupid's little helper, no?"

"He looks like a wild horse," Francesca said, and then she wrinkled her nose. "He smells like one too."

Stone remembered Tomahawk tied in front of the Last Chance Saloon. "Got to go," he said, rising from his chair. "Thanks for the mescal."

"Have one more?"

"Don't mind if I do."

Stone filled his glass half-full, guzzled it down, wiped his mouth with the back of his hand, and staggered across the restaurant, passing a stout Mexican stuffing goat brains into his mouth.

Stone dropped heavily at the table with Duvall and Blakemore.

"What did the greaser want?" asked Blakemore.

"I've got to look at my horse."

Duvall said, "I thought we was goin' to Madam Lazonga's? That old cayuse of yours can wait a few more minutes."

Stone tried to get up, but his legs wouldn't obey the command. He felt numb, as if his head were expanding.

"C'mon," Duvall said with a grin, pulling him to his feet.

The three gringos stomped out of Pancho's and landed on a deserted street not far from the downtown saloon district. They found their bearings, stuffed their hands into their pockets, and walked with heads down toward the Gypsy woman's parlor.

Stone felt as if he were a puppet, and the man pulling the strings had gone home for the night. The wear and tear of too many years of hard drinking, plus too much fighting, and his share of hardship were taking their toll. *I've got to get some rest*, he said to himself. *I've got to regroup and rebuild my reserves.*

"The old humbug is on this street," Blakemore said. "If she don't give me my money back, I'll stuff that crystal ball down her throat."

Stone thought he should bring Veronika a gift, but he had no money. Maybe he could walk to the edge of town and pick some flowers.

"There's her house, but it looks closed for the night."

"We'll open 'er up!" Duvall said.

The house was darkened, and the sign gone from the window. Duvall pounded his fist on the door. "Open up!" he hollered. "I want to know my fortune!"

There was silence for a few minutes, and Stone rolled a cigarette. "Maybe we ought to forget about this."

"I want to see the look on her face when she sees all of us together," Blakemore said.

The door swung open, and an old man with long white mustaches stood there in his long underwear, aiming a double-barreled shotgun at Blakemore's head.

Blakemore raised his hands. "Whoa! Just a minute!"

Duvall stepped forward. "I come to see Madam Lazonga, to git my fortune told."

"Who's Madam Lazonga?"

"The old Gypsy woman who lives here and tells fortunes for twenty-five cents a shot."

"I live with my cat, and you knock on my door again this time of night, it'll be you and me to the bitter end."

The old man slammed the door.

"Maybe," said Duvall, "this is the wrong house."

"Looks like the right one to me," Blakemore said, pushing his forage cap to the back of his head. "What do you think, Johnny Reb?"

Stone was sure it was the Gypsy's house, but where was the gypsy? Then he remembered Veronika. It was time to pay his call. "See you boys back at the bunkhouse."

Stone wheeled, nearly fell over, and scuffed down the street, heading toward the Barlowe House, the tips of his fingers in his front pockets, the cigarette dangling out of the corner of his mouth. Maybe Madam Lazonga lived on another street, and they'd made a mistake.

He recalled the flowers, and swerved into an alley, heading for the open prairie at the edge of town, stumbling, bumping into a shovel and knocking it over, it clanged as it struck the ground, and he stepped over it, only to fall onto a wheelbarrow, painfully bruising his knee, and the wheelbarrow tipped over, depositing him upon the ground.

He looked up and saw flowers growing out of a window box. He plucked a handful of them, trimmed off the roots with the blade of his Apache knife, and arranged a tasteful bouquet.

"Who the hell's out there!" bellowed a man's voice, and Stone smiled like a fox as he tiptoed out of the alley and back to the sidewalk.

He made his way toward the center of town, and climbed the stairs of the Barlowe House, holding the bouquet in front of him like a trooper carrying the guidon on parade. The lobby was deserted except for a man dressed like a dude, wearing a stovepipe hat, asleep on a chair in the corner. Stone climbed the stairs to the third floor, thinking of the beauteous Veronika.

He walked down the hall, the cigarette still hanging out of his mouth, his eyes nearly closed, knees bent, his shoulders scraping the walls on both sides. He didn't feel romantic, but was sure he'd get in the mood as soon as they touched. He felt himself coming back to life as he approached the door marked 321.

He removed his hat, took a deep breath, and knocked on the door. There was no response, and he thought maybe she'd fallen asleep, so he banged again.

Footsteps approached, and he readied himself, flowers in his hand, Lancelot visiting fair Guinevere. The door opened, and

Stone saw a sleepy man with a large swooping mustache with the ends turned up, a shaven head, and a maroon silk robe.

"*Ja?*" the man asked, gazing with surprise at the bouquet of flowers in front of his face.

"I think I have the wrong room," Stone stuttered.

"Who vere you looking for?"

"A lady named Guinevere."

"Try the whorehouse."

The door slammed in Stone's face, who looked again to make sure the number on the door was 321, and it was. Someone had arrived before he; you could never trust a woman. Stone dropped the bouquet of flowers in the middle of the hallway and skulked toward the stairs. He didn't know what happened, and didn't care. He was exhausted deep in his body, and all he wanted to do was sleep.

He walked out the door and made his way over the sidewalk, heading for the Last Chance Saloon. The street was dark and deserted, and only a few horses were tied to the rails; most everybody had gone to bed long ago.

He thought of Marie, Cassandra, Madam Lazonga, Veronika, and his mother back in South Carolina before the war. He realized that he, as Don Emilio said, had spent his life trying to make women love him. Why do men go to war? Because the women are watching.

He spotted a cowboy sprawled in the gutter, a pint of whiskey near his hand. Glancing in both directions, Stone picked up the whiskey and held it in the moonlight. It was three-quarters full, so he removed the cork and took a few swallows, then hissed through his teeth, replaced the cork, and placed the bottle into his back pocket. Raising his eyes to the sidewalk, he saw a hatless figure standing in the shadows.

"Who's there?" he asked, lowering his hands to his six-guns.

"Stealin' another man's whiskey?" Ephraim asked, a taunting note in his voice. "Why, Massa John, I'm surprised at you."

Stone approached silently, while Ephraim stood in the shadows.

"What're you doing here?" Stone asked.

"I can go wherever I want, Massa John. It's a free country now. But I still gotta say *massa* to all the po' white trash, so's they leaves old Ephraim alone, but I guess things have got pretty bad when the boss man's son has got to rob whiskey from drunken cowboys lying in the gutter."

Stone cocked his head to the side and looked at him, and Ephraim, exactly his height, was packed with muscles that strained against his tight blue shirt.

"I thought there was someplace nigras went," Stone said, "so white men don't have to look at them."

"There is, Massa John, but sometimes I likes to see how the white man lives"—he winked—"and the white women."

"Don't push too far."

"I say somethin' wrong, Massa John? I'm so sorry. I hopes you'll forgive this poor old darky, but I'm a man like you, and feel what you feel, and want the same things you want. I bet you looked at some purty nigra women in yer time, and had thoughts you didn't want to tell nobody."

"You got that one wrong."

Ephraim chortled. "Then you ain't yer daddy's son, because your daddy liked to visit the slave quarters at night, when your momma was asleep, and he liked 'em young, 'round fourteen or fifteen, so don't turn up yer nose at me, Massa Stone, I know more than you think."

"You're a liar!"

"Am I? Then where the hell you think yer high yeller slaves come from? Let me tell you, Massa John—you had lots of brothers and sisters out there in the fields, and they didn't come from heaven, they came out'n yer daddy's pecker!"

Stone hit him with everything he had, but Ephraim dodged to the side at the last moment. Stone's fist smashed into the wall, the skin on his knuckles burst apart, and he let out a terrible scream. Ephraim hit him with a right hook to the kidney, and a left hook to his other kidney, and when Stone lowered his elbows for protection, Ephraim hooked him to the side of his head.

Stone went reeling backward, fell over the rail, and landed head first in the gutter. Ephraim stood over him. "I wanted to do that all my life!" he said. "And God, did it feel good!"

Stone dragged himself to his feet. Gone were the fatigue and drunken wooziness, because nothing in the world is as purifying as a solid left hook to the brainpan. He stood, looked at Ephraim, and Ephraim fixed his two eyes on him.

"Never figured you was much, under that sickly white skin," Ephraim said. "Do me a favor, Massa John, and punch me again, so I'll have the excuse to take another inch off'n yer hide."

Stone raised his fists and advanced. He'd been caught off guard, that's all. Many times in his life he'd picked himself up off the floor and gone on to kick the shit out of the man who'd put him down, and it looked as though this was going to be that kind of fight.

Stone closed the distance between him and Ephraim, leaned to the left, leaned to the right, and let fly a probing left jab, to see what Ephraim would do with it, but Ephraim slipped it easily and moved inside to work Stone's body again. Stone took one short step to the left, simultaneously launching an uppercut, because Ephraim had been holding his head low.

His fist connected with the point of Ephraim's chin, and Ephraim's head snapped up. Then Stone fired his own kidney shot, and air spewed out of Ephraim's mouth, but he stood his ground, punched Stone in the stomach once, twice, three times, and then it felt as if ten bales of cotton landed on Ephraim, as Stone landed a chopping right to his temple.

Ephraim raised his fist to protect that side of his head, and took a step back to clear his head, but Stone stayed close, feinted a left hook, looked for an angle, found it, and fired a right hook that struck Ephraim on his wide nostrils.

Blood spurted out, and Stone thought he had his man. He lunged in for the kill, but was too eager, and off balance, and Ephraim saw his chance, stepping to the side and dancing away. Stone found himself facing the open sidewalk.

Ephraim wiped the blood from his nose, and his eyes were ablaze with anger.

"What you run for?" Stone asked, and this time the ridicule was in his voice. "Can't stand up to a white man?"

"I've hated you all my life, Massa John, and that little blond gal you used to go with, the one who used to wear all the pretty dresses, we got together one night and . . ."

Stone screamed bloody blue murder, and both of them came together on the sidewalk, throwing punches from all angles, smacking each other in their faces, winging shots at each other's torsos, and half the punches were wild. Neither would back up or move to the side. Blind rage had taken over, and they were trying to beat each other to death.

Stone felt his nose crack and his lower lip burst open. The two o'clock express from Atlanta crashed into his left ear, but he never faltered as he hurled punch after punch at Ephraim, and Ephraim's left eye was a purple plum, completely closed, blood pouring from his mouth and nose.

They hurled and received shots that would've taken out other men, and Stone knew victory would go to the one who dug in his heels and held out longest. He regretted all the booze he'd drunk, and all the wear and tear he'd put on his body, because he simply *could not* lose to this man.

A blow hit Stone in the middle of his chest, and he couldn't breathe. He covered, took a step back, and saw it was the best move he could make. Ephraim rushed forward blindly, and he was wide open.

A vicious jab to the mouth stopped Ephraim cold in his tracks, and a right cross sent him sprawling back into the wall. Instead of falling, as Stone thought he would, Ephraim bounced off the wall and came back at him with a straight right, but Stone ducked under it, darted to the side, and pounded him on the nose again.

Ephraim dropped flat on his face and lay still for a few moments, then opened his one good eye and looked up at Stone who said, "I ought to kill you."

"For what I said about that lil' blond gal?" Ephraim replied, his face streaked with blood. "What if I told you she loved everything I gave her, and even begged—yes *begged*—this darky for more!"

Stone kicked Ephraim's head, and Ephraim grabbed his ankle, twisting hard. Stone lost his balance and fell to the boardwalk, receiving several splinters into his hand on the way down, and Ephraim was on him in an instant, whacking, jabbing, bashing, and kicking. They rolled over and around, trying to kill each other with their bare hands. Their faces were inches apart, and they could smell each other's bodies and breath, as they rolled off the sidewalk into the muck and horseshit in the street.

A window opened above them. "What the hell's going on down there!"

Stone and Ephraim looked up and saw an old woman wearing a nightcap, holding a sawed-off double-barreled shotgun in her hands.

"You boys do that someplace else!" she hollered. "I got to get up in the mornin'."

A door opened in the next house, and a young barefoot man stepped onto the sidewalk, peering at Stone and Ephraim.

"Is that a white man and a nigra fightin' over there?"

Ephraim bolted down the nearest alley. Stone raised himself and brushed the muck off his clothes. Negro men had been lynched in Texas for far less than daring to fight with a white man.

The young man walked toward him. "What was that all about?"

"Drinking too much," Stone replied.

The woman in the second-story window shouted: "God-damned cowboys—all they want to do is fight!"

She slammed the window, leaving Stone with the young man gazing at Stone's mangled face. "Maybe you should see a doctor."

"Don't believe in 'em," Stone replied, walking away.

His legs were unsteady and he was punch-drunk as he made his way toward the Last Chance Saloon. His ears were ringing, and he'd taken some terrible shots. Stopping at the curb, he spit a mouthful of blood into the gutter.

It was the first time he'd ever gone at it with a Negro, and was surprised by how well Ephraim had done, but the fight wasn't over yet. They'd get it on again some other time, where there'd be no one to stop them.

Stone ground his teeth together, recalling what Ephraim said about Marie. It was a lie, calculated to piss him off, because Marie would never look twice at any other man, never mind a Negro slave.

Or would she? Stone knew there were depths to that little blonde he'd never fathomed, her strange smiles, the wicked things she'd say and do in the heat of love—where had she learned them? Sometimes he'd had his doubts about Marie, but then he shook his head and laughed, because she'd been rebellious, but not rebellious enough to risk her reputation and that of her family for a few fleeting moments with a common field slave.

Stone had been told from the day he was born that Negroes weren't as good as white men. Ephraim's remark was a defilement of white women, but Stone knew, from bitter experience, how capricious Cupid could be. Anything could happen between the sheets, and he had to admit to himself that he'd seen saucy Negro slave girls in tight dresses who'd evoked in him the deepest sentiments of lust.

The part about his father, he refused to consider. It simply couldn't be. Not his father, although he'd had many friends whose fathers had bedded their slave women, and people said Thomas Jefferson kept a slave girl.

Stone looked down the street to the Last Chance Saloon, and saw only three horses tied to the rail. His heart went out to poor Tomahawk, alone and unfed for so long, the unfortunate hard-working animal, who'd never let him down, who did whatever was asked of him, whereas Stone neglected him every day, treating him like a thing that had no needs.

Stone quickened his pace, and something hurt his posterior. He reached his hand around, and found his pants soaking wet. The pint of whiskey had broken, soaking whiskey into the cloth, cutting his skin. He stopped, leaned against a doorpost, and carefully picked glass out of his back pocket, but cut his finger and thumb before he finished, and there still were a few pieces he couldn't get out.

He stumbled down the street toward the Last Chance Saloon, and looked a wreck, his clothes torn, and blood all over his face, dripping from his finger and thumb. Approaching the front of the saloon, he saw Tomahawk standing between the other horses.

Tomahawk gazed at him without reproach. He'd been through this before, and it did no good. The man reached into his pocket, came out with some coins, and staggered into the saloon.

Stone thought he might as well have one last drink for the road. It would use up his remaining money, but that was all-right, because tomorrow he'd start a new slate at the Triangle

Spur, and begin his study of the Texas cattle industry.

He bellied up to the bar, tossed his coins upon it, and said, "Whiskey!"

The bartender, dozing next to the cash box, opened his eyes and poured whiskey into a glass. Stone paid him and carried the whiskey to a table where he could sit with his back to the wall and his face to the door.

He didn't have any difficulty finding such a table, because most of the tables were empty. It was nearly three o'clock in the morning on a weekday night, and everybody had to work the next day, including Stone, and he knew it was going to be murder in the morning at the Triangle Spur.

I've got to get serious about life, he said to himself. *I'm killing myself with drinking and fooling around. I'm liable to wind up one of those old drunks I see in the gutter of every town I've ever been in. I used to be an officer, for Christ's sake. Wade Hampton himself asked for my opinions at staff meetings. I have abilities and intelligence, when I'm sober. I've got to dry out and be a man again.*

A man in a plaid shirt stumbled and tripped through the swinging doors, nearly falling on his face, and Stone stiffened in his chair. It was one of the bodyguards he'd encountered at Veronika's dressing room earlier in the evening.

The man in the plaid shirt staggered toward the bar, leaned against it, and hollered at the top of his lungs: "Bartender— I'm a-looking fer a man about this tall"—he held his hand at Stone's height—"built thick in the chest and sportin' two Colts—you seen him around?"

"That him over there?" the bartender asked, pointing at Stone.

The man in the plaid shirt spun around, reaching for his six-gun, and Stone already was on his feet, drawing both his Colts, pulling the triggers.

His first barrage demolished two bottles of whiskey behind the bar, and then plaid shirt fired, his bullet smacking into the wall three feet from Stone's left ear.

Stone fired another volley, sending a spittoon flying into the air, covering the bartender with slop, cigar butts, tobacco juice, and an old rag. His other bullets provided ventilation for the mirror behind the bar.

Plaid shirt took careful aim, and his bullet punctured the floorboard near Stone's left toe. Stone tried to settle down and pick his shots, although it wasn't easy to settle down when bullets were flying around.

He triggered his Colts, and plaid shirt's hat flew off his head, but plaid shirt held his gun with both hands and fired a careful shot at Stone's heart. An *olla* jar, hanging from the ceiling, exploded into bits above Stone's head.

The bartender laughed. "I never seen two worse shots in my life! You cowboys couldn't hit a bull's ass with a banjo!"

The absurdity of the situation struck Stone, and he giggled in spite of himself. His knees wobbled from side to side, his arms were like overcooked macaroni, and he no longer could aim his guns effectively.

But the man in the plaid shirt had his legs spread apart and sighted down the barrel of his gun once more, while Stone's body was wracked with uncontrollable perverse mirth. Stone closed his eyes and waited for the bullet that would send him to that big ranch in the sky when he heard: *click!*

Plaid shirt's gun had jammed, and he lost his temper, throwing it at the floor. It exploded on contact, and a bullet whizzed into the wall next to a drunk passed out on his table who didn't budge an inch.

Now plaid shirt's sense of humor took hold of him, and he dropped to his knees, hugging his sides, howling with laughter.

Tears rolled down the bartender's face as he filled three glasses of whiskey in the middle of the bar. "Shootin' that bad deserves the special booby prize, but since we ain't got one, how's about drinks on the house!"

Stone holstered his guns and moved unsteadily toward the free whiskey. The man in the plaid shirt joined him, and they raised their glasses in the air.

"Here's to the two worst gunfighters I've ever seen!" the bartender roared.

They drained their glasses dry.

"You gents sure are fun!" said the bartender. "Let's have one more once!"

He filled the glasses again, and they guzzled the liquid down. The bartender walked away, carrying the bottle back to its assigned spot, next to his Smith & Wesson.

Stone and the man in the plaid shirt looked at each other and realized they were drunken violent sons of bitches, and not much could be done about it.

"Sorry I knifed your friend," Stone said, "but you know how it is."

Plaid shirt nodded. "He weren't my friend, and once he cheated me at cards, but you weren't smart when you went to that lady's room, because she's another man's woman, and he ain't nobody to fool with. I'm talkin about Count Von Falkenheim, who owns the Diamond D."

Stone recalled the man with the strange, crooked, upturned mustache who'd answered Veronika's door. "Fuck him if he can't take a joke."

"He fired me," plaid shirt said, "and it was the best job I ever had. Din't have to ride no range, din't have to punch no cattle, all I had to do is sit around and proteck that woman from cowboys like you who think you can git some of what she's sittin' on."

"Almost did," Stone said. "What's your name?"

"Haliday."

Stone placed his bloody hand on Haliday's shoulder. "How'd you like to go to Kansas?"

"What's there I can't get cheaper in Texas?"

"The Triangle Spur is sendin' their herd up the trail. I'm going, and you can too."

Haliday made a rough motion with his hand. "I wouldn't go anywheres with them cowboys. Their ramrod's a drunk, the *segundo* is off his rocker, and nobody else knows anything about cattle except an eighteen-year-old kid who don't smoke, drink, swear, or do anything wrong. My friend, you don't go up the trail with a bunch of dumb galoots like that."

"I am," Stone said, "and they got an awfully good cook."

"Boss lady's purty too. Don't know what she sees in that old loudmouth, though."

"What makes you say that?"

"Old enough to be her father, for chrissakes. Can you picture them in bed together? It's enough to make a man puke."

"Love doesn't make sense, Haliday. Haven't you ever been in love?"

"A long time ago. Me and two of my friends ran across this gal in the woods, and she was a little tetched in the head, so we just sweet-talked her a little, and pretty soon she gave us what we wanted."

Stone felt a wave of fatigue break over him like an ocean wave. He pushed himself away from the bar and said, "Not feeling so good. Got to lie down. Talk to you some other time."

Stone wheeled and shuffled toward the door, a stain of blood on the back of his pants where the glass had cut his haunch. He pushed open the doors and stepped onto the sidewalk, looking directly into the face of Tomahawk, who gazed at him mournfully, with an expression that seemed to say: When are you going home, pal?

"You poor son of a bitch," Stone said, patting Tomahawk's forehead. "You deserve better than me, but I do the best I can. Let's go to the prairie, where a man's a man and a horse is a horse."

Stone climbed onto the saddle and pulled the reins around gently. Tomahawk headed out of town, his head bobbing up and down, and Stone wrapped both hands around the pommel, so he wouldn't fall off. He drooped in the saddle, as deep fatigue came over him.

He felt as if he didn't have an ounce of strength left in his body, and his mind functioned with only the smallest glimmer of consciousness. He hurt all over, thanks to Ephraim, but Ephraim would be feeling pain too. It wouldn't be over until one of them was lying on the ground and the other wasn't.

In Stone's drowsiness, Ephraim was a bad dream drifting through his mind. Who could've imagined one day a man's slave would return to give him grief? Stone thought back to the days of Albemarle, magnolia trees lining the paths, the parties, dancing, great feasts. At night he slept on a big feather mattress, and never worked a day in his life until he went to West Point.

He saw himself marching across the plain at West Point, in the ranks with the cadets, saluting with his sword the commandant. He'd never realized it at the time, but they'd been the best days of his life.

Then came the war, bombs bursting around him, incredible carnage, screams of men, blood flowing in rivulets on the battlefield. They'd shot him and sliced him, done everything they could to him, and he had survived, but for what?

Something was moving on the prairie, and Stone leaned toward it, his eyes nearly closed. It was Veronika beckoning to him out of the night, dancing lewdly on the grassy swales, shaking, wiggling, snapping her fingers over her head, and she was completely naked.

He reached toward her, and at that moment everything hit him at once. His system was overloaded with alcohol and excesses of all kinds, and he blacked out, leaning over perilously, falling out of the saddle.

He crashed into the ground and lay still, his face buried in the dirt at the bottom of the trail. Tomahawk looked down at him with bitter disappointment, but this wasn't the first time it had happened. All Tomahawk's owners had been cowboys, and it was all he knew.

He looked at the empty prairie, and there were wild herds of horses he could join, and live free, but he'd never lived free in his life, he'd been born and raised on a ranch, fed by cowboys and then broken by them at an early age. He'd grown up feeling a strange sense of brotherhood with cowboys, and besides, how'd he get the saddle off?

Tomahawk sniffed Stone, and wrinkled his nostrils at the alcohol fumes. They were in the middle of the trail, and somebody might come along. Tomahawk inserted his snout underneath Stone and rolled him onto his back. Then he grabbed Stone's gunbelt in his teeth and dragged him off the trail into a hollow behind a hill, where they couldn't be seen from the trail.

Tomahawk dropped his head and munched grass as Stone snored and wheezed beneath the big full moon in the endless western sky.

5

CASSANDRA ROLLED OUT of bed at dawn, careful not to awaken her husband. She dressed in the darkness, then went to the kitchen to issue her daily instructions to the staff.

Then she sat at her desk, beneath the framed portrait of Stonewall Jackson, and looked at the figures again, but ten thousand dollars still were gone. She felt a mild stab of panic in her breast.

Breakfast was served, and she returned to the dining room, where she sipped coffee, but was unable to eat anything. When she was on her second cup, her husband entered the dining room, kissed her cheek, and sat opposite her, then lay his napkin onto his lap.

"I'm bored," Whiteside complained. "Maybe I'll go to town."

"I've got to do some banking," she said. "Perhaps we can go in together?"

"If you like."

He didn't sound enthusiastic about going to town with her, but she understood sometimes a man needed to be alone. No one person could hope to satisfy all of another person's needs, she told herself.

"We're having a little financial problem," she told him. "Ten thousand dollars is missing from our accounts."

He held his hand in the air and smiled indulgently. "You

take care of the clerical work, please—I have more important things to worry about."

The maid brought a platter of eggs, potatoes, grits and ham, placing it before Whiteside, and he dug into it with his knife and fork, ignoring Cassandra. She decided to go to San Antone tomorrow, and have one of the cowboys drive the buckboard. She'd speak with Mr. Dohenney at the bank, and maybe he could locate the ten thousand dollars.

That much money just doesn't disappear, Cassandra thought. *Where is it?*

The sun seared Stone's eyeballs as he awakened, lying on his back. He moved and felt a sharp pain in his left kidney, and his face ached as if flesh had been ripped away.

He groaned, and Tomahawk munched a mouthful of greens, gazing solemnly at him. Stone raised himself to his knees and rolled a cigarette, then got to his feet and looked around. He didn't remember coming to this hill, and was pleased to realize he'd had the good sense to get off the trail, even though he was drunk and evidently had blacked out. *A man's inner common sense will always take care of him, even if he's drunk,* Stone thought.

Stone walked toward Tomahawk, uncinched the saddle, and pulled it away. "Sorry you had to keep that on all night," Stone said apologetically. "Won't happen again."

The hell it won't, Tomahawk thought, able to breathe more easily now, and he returned to his breakfast of nutritious grass. Stone sat with his saddlebags and looked inside. He found a few moldy biscuits, a rotten chunk of bacon, and a can of beans. He threw the biscuits and bacon away, opened the can of beans, and ate them with a spoon. They were cold and slimy, with the flavor of coal oil.

He had a headache, and something serious appeared wrong with his nose. He touched it with his finger, and it jiggled. He realized his nose had been broken by Ephraim.

He tossed the empty can of beans over his shoulder and searched within the cavernous depths of his saddlebags for coffee beans, finding a dirty pair of socks, his poncho, and then the beans wrapped in oilcloth inside the used lard tin he used for a coffeepot.

He built a fire, ground the beans between two rocks, and dumped them into the lard tin along with water from his canteen. Soon the water was boiling, and the fragrance of hot coffee filled the prairie air. Stone let it boil for a while, because he liked his coffee thick as axle grease and unadulterated by milk or sugar.

He sipped the coffee while watching a family of prairie rats nibbling the bacon and biscuits he'd thrown away, and realized other men were doctors and lawyers, bankers and ranchers, and he was just another prairie rat.

I've got to sober up and learn the ranching business. If I work hard, and keep regular hours, I'll be healthy again, and then I'll be able to do anything I want. The only person I have to worry about is Ephraim, but I'll just stay away from him. I've got better things to do.

Stone wanted to feel strong again. If he had to fight, he wanted to be in first-rate condition, so he wouldn't have to take the punishment he'd taken from Ephraim, and if he had to use his guns, he wanted his aim to be accurate, unlike the shameless performance he'd given last night at the Last Chance Saloon. If Haliday had been sober, Stone would've been killed. No question about it. *I can't let that happen again.*

Stone glanced at the sun, and it was nearing high noon. He tossed the old lard tin into his saddlebags, kicked dirt over the fire, then walked toward Tomahawk, to begin his journey to the Triangle Spur.

Count Von Falkenheim and Veronika enjoyed a late break-fast in her suite at the Barlowe House. They looked out the windows at wagons and riders on the wide avenue, and occasionally they heard a shout, or a peal of laughter, or a gunshot, as an enthusiastic cowboy put on an impromptu display of marksmanship.

Von Falkenheim didn't dress like a cowboy, because he considered cowboys workmen, and he was no workman. He was a Prussian gentleman, a former captain in the imperial guards, and still dressed like a military man, with riding jodphurs, knee-length highly polished black boots, and a high-necked beige shirt with billowing sleeves.

"By the vay," he said to Veronika, "some fellow vas here

last night looking for you. Voke me up. Do you know anything about it?"

She wore a red silk dressing gown, and no cosmetics. Her straight black hair was smoothly combed, and she already had taken her morning bath, with him.

"Probably another drunken cowboy," she said casually. "They are all in love vith the woman who dances vithout many clothes."

"Vhat presumption," Von Falkenheim said. "This fellow appeared so drunk he could barely stand, undt he had veeds in his hand. He nearly fainted vhen I opened the door. Vonder how he found out your room number?"

"It is no secret."

He gazed at her, and twirled the end of his mustache. "I am sure you understand that if I ever found you vith another fellow, I vould haf to kill him."

She placed her palm on his forearm. "You need not worry, my dear Volfgang. If ve vere back in Munich, then perhaps you might haf reason for concern, but I assure you, I am not interested in any of these drunken cowboy fools. Vhat do you think I am?"

"A woman who loves to make love."

"But only with you, Volfie dear."

"I hope you mean that, my little vixen, because I never haf shrunk from spilling blood in matters of honor, undt that is vhat this is, you understand."

"It is too early to argue, Volfie. Perhaps later in the day you can tie me up undt beat me, but not now, all right?"

He smiled as he sliced into his breakfast steak. "Actually, I am sure it was a mistake. I cannot imagine you hafing anything to do with such a man. He vas filthy, obviously little more than a tramp. You may leave me someday, my little minx, but not for an ignorant cowboy. I am confident that your taste has become more elevated than that in the years since you haf known me."

"My taste has *alvays* been more elevated than that, my dear count. You need never worry about that."

She sliced into her breakfast steak, aware she'd had a close call last night. The count had come to town unexpectedly, and it was a good thing Stone hadn't been there. She now realized she'd been flirting with danger, and danger called her bluff. It was all so silly, now that she thought of it, but the cowboy had been appealing for a moment, with his run-down boozy charm, and that smile that would melt an iceberg in the dark.

A man's smile always had been important to Veronika, and Wolfgang scored highly in that department also. Wolfgang was the very model of a Prussian officer, with all the dash and glamour, ready to fight at a moment's notice, but always a gentleman, with impeccable manners and an air of superiority so thick nothing could penetrate it.

He drained his coffee cup and placed it on the saucer. "I am afraid I must be going. Lots to do at the ranch. You understand."

He put on his black leather coat, his cowboy hat, and lit a thin cigar imported from Holland. Then he stopped and regarded himself in her full-length mirror, admiring the cut and tailoring of his clothing, and his handsome mustached visage.

He returned to her, kissed her lips, and then spun and walked to the door, opening it and pausing at the edge of the oriental rug.

"Remember vhat I told you, *schatzchen*. If you are ever unfaithful to me, I vill kill your lover, no matter vhat it costs, or how long it takes. And I vill rub your face in his blood. Clear?"

"Very," she replied.

He stepped into the hallway, closed the door, and was gone.

The cowboys were seated at the long table in the bunkhouse, eating stew and biscuits, when Stone arrived. He saw Duvall and Blakemore among them, the *segundo* at the head of the table, and beside him, standing on the table, was the dog, growling softly and staring at the *segundo*'s food. All at once the *segundo* raised his arm and batted the dog off the table, and it yelped as it hit the floor. The *segundo* laughed as he reached for another biscuit.

Stone's eyes fell on Ephraim, sitting beside the stove. Ephraim appeared as if he'd fallen face first into a sausage grinder, with huge welts and cuts all over his face, and portions of his skin had turned purple, while other portions were an iridescent green. His left eye was puffed into a bubble and completely closed.

Stone walked past him without a word and filled a bowl with stew, then sat opposite Blakemore and Duvall.

"What happened to you?" Blakemore asked, examining Stone's battered visage. "You look like you've been in a hatchet fight, and you was the only one without a hatchet."

"Fell down a flight of stairs," Stone said.

"Some people can't walk straight after they gets a few drinks in 'em, looks like."

"I'll never drink again," Stone muttered.

"That's what she said when the bed broke."

Ben Thorpe, the young cowboy with freckles on his nose, had finished eating and was walking past a window, on the way toward his bunk, when he happened to glance outside. "Holy bejesus!"

He gazed through the window and saw, advancing toward the bunkhouse, a bony old man with a long gray beard and a beat-up hat whose brim had a chunk torn out of it.

"They're hirin' the dregs as it is," Thorpe said, "but this one looks like somethin' that ought to be under six feet of dirt."

With a groan, Thorpe lay on his bunk and covered his eyes with his hands. Everybody stared at the door as footsteps approached outside. Then suddenly the door was flung open and the old man stepped inside the bunkhouse.

"Where's the grub!" he demanded, standing on skinny bowed legs.

Stone stared at him in amazement, because their paths had crossed before. It was Ray Slipchuck, the old demented alcoholic stagecoach driver.

Slipchuck's vision was poor under the best of circumstances, but it was dark in the bunkhouse, and he narrowed his eyes as he tried to focus on the food.

"Over here," said Ephraim. "Help yourself, cowboy."

Slipchuck swaggered toward the pot of stew and filled a bowl to the brim, his eyes glittering with hunger. Then he carried the bowl to the table and filled his mouth, chewing with the few teeth he had left, and gumming the rest.

Stone said, "I thought buzzards die when they get old, but

I guess they just become cowpokes in Texas."

Slipchuck looked in the direction of the voice, and his lips turned up in a smile. "Well I'll be a horn-swaggled son of a bitch!"

Both men arose, walked around the table, and shook hands heartily.

"Johnny my boy!" Slipchuck hollered. "You're a sight for these poor old eyes! Never thought I'd see you again! Heard outlaws killed you in Clarksdale, or what the hell ever was the name of that town we was in?"

"You were so drunk, Slipchuck, you didn't even know who you were."

"Still don't," Slipchuck replied. "Been a lost child ever since that stage line I worked for went belly up." Slipchuck shook his head as he returned to his stew. "It ain't easy for an older man to git a job these days. When I was a young man, drivin' stagecoaches all over God's creation, people respected me wherever I went. I could git a job anywheres just like that"— he snapped his finger—"but now they don't want an old feller workin' for 'em, although I'm still as good as ever, and maybe better. You know that, Johnny. We made a run together."

"Finest stagecoach driver I ever saw," Stone said. "Played that team of horses as if it were a violin."

Slipchuck beamed as he stuffed stew into his mouth.

The *segundo* leaned toward him and grimaced. "You know anything about cows?"

"Young feller," Slipchuck replied, "I was herdin' cattle when you was just an itch in yer daddy's jeans."

"We're goin' all the way to Kansas, Pops. Think you can make it that far?"

"If you can make it, I can make it."

"We'll see about that. There's many a cowboy buried on them plains, and quite a few have been drowned in them rivers, so keep yer eyes open and yer powder dry."

"I'll pull my weight," Slipchuck told him. "Always have and always will."

The door to the bunkhouse opened, and Truscott entered, wearing his slouched cowboy hat, a rawhide vest, and wide floppy leggins. Leather work gloves were on his hands, and he smoked a bent cigarette.

He announced the work assignments for tomorrow. Most of the men would continue forming the herd, a few would stay back at the ranch for chores and general farm work, and then he looked at Stone.

"You'll take the boss lady into town. Have the buckboard in front of the main house at eight o'clock in the morning."

"Can't somebody else take care of that, Ramrod?" Stone replied. "I'd rather work with the herd, get some experience with cattle."

"I just told you yer job, Stone. You don't like it, you can light a shuck on out of here." Truscott looked at Stone coldly, then advanced toward him, stopping on the other side of the table. "Let's you and me understand each other, Stone. I don't know what you were in the war, and don't much give a damn. But while you're ridin' for this brand, you'll foller my orders, and I don't want no back talk, questions, arguments, or bullshit. Understand?"

"Anything you say."

Truscott walked out of the bunkhouse, and everyone breathed easier. Stone wondered why he'd been picked to escort Cassandra Whiteside to San Antone. That was the last place he wanted to go, and she was the last person he wanted to be with.

The *segundo* looked at him, a leer in his eyes. "I think she's lookin' fer a good hot screw about now, and maybe you'll be the lucky cowboy."

Stone decided not to respond, and maybe the *segundo* would let go, but he didn't.

"You and me can switch," the *segundo* said. "She'll know what a real man is when I'm finished with her,'stead of that one-armed old windbag she's married to."

Stone didn't like to hear a lady spoken about that way, but decided he'd had enough fighting last night to keep him satisfied for at least a year. He sipped coffee and leaned back in his chair, determined to avoid any provocation.

"You ain't gonna try to slip it to the boss lady, are you, Stone?"

Stone gazed into his cup of coffee.

"Asked you a question, Stone."

"Don't think I will," Stone replied, "but if I do, you'll be the first to know, *segundo*."

"Don't leave out no details, like what her pants smell like and such."

Stone arose from the table and rinsed his coffee cup in the bucket. No matter where he went, people wouldn't leave him alone. All he wanted was a little peace and quiet, and the opportunity to learn the cattle business. It didn't seem like so much to ask.

He walked to his bunk, unbuttoned his shirt, and took the picture of Marie out of the pocket. She'd been the most important part of his life, and he'd never see her again. "So long, kid," he said, affecting a flippancy he didn't feel. "It's been good to know you."

He tossed her picture into his saddlebags, along with his dirty clothes and his emergency can of beans. Then he took off his shirt and went outside to wash.

It was late afternoon, and the sun sank toward the horizon. A faint breeze carried the sweet vegetative fragrance of prairie past his nostrils. He poured a pitcher of water into the basin, and washed his upper torso. Then he reached for the towel.

The door to the privy opened, and Ephraim came out, buttoning his pants. He and Stone looked at each other, and their faces bore mute testimony to their fierce battle. Stone recalled what Ephraim had said about his father, and felt the rage return with all its high-power electricity.

Stone stood in Ephraim's path, and Ephraim came straight at him. Stone wasn't about to get out of Ephraim's way, and it looked as though Ephraim wouldn't step to the side either. *Here we go again,* Stone thought.

Stone spread his legs for a good solid grip on the ground, and balled his fists. Ephraim's lips were pressed together, his nostrils flared. The inevitable collision would take place in three seconds and then it would be punch and kick until somebody went down.

The back door to the bunkhouse opened, and they heard the *segundo*'s voice. "Hey, burrhead, where you been, boy? You better git in here and fix another pot of coffee, or I'll kick yer black ass!"

Ephraim's countenance changed, and he became the shuffling dumb Negro again. "Yessir. Ah'll be right there!"

His body bent submissively, Ephraim walked toward the rear

door, and as he entered the bunkhouse, the *segundo* kicked him in the rear end. "Damned lazy burrhead—never around when you want him." Then the *segundo* looked at Stone. "If'n it's a bath you want, there's a stream over yonder!"

Stone thought that a fine idea. He walked toward the bunkhouse, and Slipchuck came out, emitting a burp.

"Johnny boy," he said. "When I saw you in there, I couldn't believe me eyes. Just goes to show you, I'm like a bad penny, allus showin' up."

"You're no bad penny," Stone said, slapping him on the shoulder. "You're the best damned stagecoach driver I ever saw, but you stink like hell. Come on down to the river and take a bath."

Slipchuck waved his long bony finger back and forth. "I got my own ideas about that, Johnny. To my way of thinkin', too much bathin' weakens a man. Washes away his manhood. Doctor told me so."

"What kind of doctor?"

"Sold rattlesnake oil from the back of a wagon. Claimed it'd cure anything. I still got some, if'n you ever feel the need."

"Hope I never feel the need, but if you don't take a bath, the other cowboys might not let you sleep in the bunkhouse tonight. You smell like a fish that's been dead for about two weeks and lying all that time in the sun."

"It's that bad, Johnny? I didn't know that. Are you sure?"

"I'm about ready to pass out, Slipchuck, and we're standing in the wind."

"If I get sick afterward, you might have to fetch my rattlesnake oil. I ain't used to this sort of thing."

"I know, Slipchuck."

They entered the bunkhouse, and Stone saw Ephraim standing at the stove. They looked at each other, and Stone could see the fierce gleam of hatred in Ephraim's eyes.

Someday we'll be alone, and nobody'll stop us, Stone thought. *Then we'll fight it out to the death.*

Ephraim's eyes replied: *I pray for that day.*

In the main house, Cassandra lay alone in bed, staring at the ceiling. She hoped Gideon hadn't been ambushed by Indians, because he hadn't yet returned from town.

Gideon stayed away from home occasionally, and she always worried about him. She knew about his shortness of breath when he exerted himself, the pain in his lower back, and he was really quite delicate, despite his robust appearance. He did no work or exercise, but no one should expect anything from a man who'd given as much to the South as he.

She had to admit that her worries were tinged with jealousy. She'd sacrificed her youth on the altar of his greatness, and if he ever were unfaithful, it would destroy her.

But that was so unthinkable it was beneath her concern. A man like Gideon wouldn't engage in cheap squalid dalliances when he owned the love and fortune of a beautiful young woman.

Cassandra knew very well that she was pretty. People had been telling her so all her life, and she'd been on dates with many young men, but they couldn't hope to compete with Gideon. They were beginning their lives, and had no accomplishments, whereas Gideon was a war hero, disabled at the height of his manhood, cast out by the cruel vicissitudes of life, and practically impoverished when she met him. And she'd saved him. If he were to cheat on her now, it would be a knife in the back.

She knew sometimes he gazed with more than passing interest at other women, and sometimes women flirted with him in the subtle ways that woman know best. But she was certain he wouldn't do anything. He had a right to look, as long as he didn't touch. Gideon was too fine a gentleman to attach scandal to his illustrious name.

Anyway, she had more important things to worry about, such as ten thousand dollars. Tomorrow morning she'd go to the bank and find out what happened to it. John Stone would drive the buckboard, an interesting road companion if she could pry him out of his shell. At least she'd feel safe with him. The other cowboys scared her to death, especially the *segundo*.

Things weren't turning out the way she'd hoped, when she left Louisiana two years ago. Gideon had said great wealth could be made easily on the frontier, but so far it'd been hard work, no success, and if that ten thousand dollars were missing, the whole operation could go down the drain.

She told herself she was worrying needlessly. The money was deposited somewhere, and the only problem was finding it. She'd know the truth tomorrow, and now the best thing to do was sleep.

She closed her eyes and tried to drift off, fretting over ten thousand dollars, Gideon's absence, and her lost innocence, as the big grandfather clock downstairs tolled midnight.

A full moon shone brightly overhead, as Slipchuck poked his head out of the bunkhouse. He hadn't been feeling well since he took that bath in the river, and now was on his way to the privy. It was like the doctor said, too much water weakened a man's vital energies.

He crossed the yard, his shirt untucked and long gray hair awry on his head. He entered the privy, constructed of unpainted posts and planks rotting away, and could see stars through gaps in the roof. Must be fun when it rains.

Slipchuck returned to the bunkhouse, thinking of how lucky he was to land the job at the Triangle Spur. Thirty bucks a month and all he could eat. Couldn't top that. And he was going to Abilene, where they had the finest whorehouses in the world. What more could a man ask?

Slipchuck noticed a sliver of light in the part of the bunkhouse occupied by Ephraim. His curiosity piqued, he thought he'd see what the cook was doing that time of night. He took a route that would carry him past Ephraim's window, and when he came close, he tiptoed the rest of the way. Maybe the Negro had a bottle, and Slipchuck could wheedle a swallow. There was nothing like whiskey to restore a man to health.

Slipchuck came to the window covered with curtains, but at the edge was a crack through which a sharp-eyed old fox could peer if he angled his head sufficiently.

Ephraim sat cross-legged in the middle of the floor, wearing a white turban and white robe, while around his neck, on a leather thong, hung the claw of a hawk.

Spread before him was a rectangle of leather covered with the shell of a turtle, the head of a coyote, the rattles of a rattlesnake, a crucifix, a candle, and several bones, some of which looked suspiciously human.

Ephraim ground leaves in a bowl, while rocking back and

forth, murmuring weird incantations. Slipchuck stared, the hair raising on the back of his neck. He'd heard rumors about strange Negro hoodoo religions, and here it was, right in front of him. Was Ephraim putting a hex on somebody?

Suddenly Ephraim glanced up at the window, an angry expression on his face, and Slipchuck pulled back, his heart frozen with fear. Slipchuck turned and fled into the darkness, his heart beating wildly, hoping Ephraim hadn't recognized him.

Slipchuck ran into the barn and dived behind a bale of hay, listening to the sound of blood pumping past his eardrums. Then he crawled into a dark corner and crouched behind a stack of barrels.

He expected Ephraim to appear at any moment, and do something terrible, but time passed and nothing happened. Gradually Slipchuck began to feel safe. Ephraim couldn't've seen him. The curtain had been nearly closed. He was being foolish.

Chortling to himself, he arose, dusted himself off, and strolled out of the barn. Got carried away for a moment. He headed toward the bunkhouse, passing a wagon, and suddenly a dark form arose behind it, reaching forward and grasping Slipchuck by the throat, squeezing the scream out of him.

Ephraim's great black head loomed in the darkness before him. "You shouldn't look in people's windows," he said. "Say something about what you just seen—I'll turn you into a bug, or a worm, or a lizard, or a pig, and you know I can do it, old man."

Slipchuck nodded. Ephraim let him go, turned, and walked back to his room, disappearing into the shadows. Slipchuck scratched his head, swallowed hard, and made his way toward the bunkhouse, wondering if he'd really seen Ephraim with those claws and bones, or if it had just been another old man's nightmare.

6

AT TEN MINUTES to eight in the morning, two matched chestnut geldings pulled a buckboard toward the main house of the Triangle Spur. Stone sat on the front seat, the reins in his hands and a cigarette dangling out of the corner of his mouth. He'd bathed, shaved, wore clean clothing, and felt like a new man, except his hands shook uncontrollably at times, but he was sure those symptoms would pass soon, and he'd be healthy again.

He pulled the horses to a halt in front of the main house, and wished he didn't have to go to San Antone. Towns were cesspools of sin and temptation for a man, and he had to stop drinking, there could be no doubt about it.

Fortunately, he had no money, and couldn't afford to drink. He'd just pass the time in the stable, or maybe even go to church and have a chat with Brother Ezra.

The door to the main house opened, and Cassandra stepped onto the porch, wearing a pastel purple dress with a flounce in back, and a matching bonnet. She walked toward the buckboard, carrying a briefcase filled with financial documents.

"Morning, ma'am," he said, tipping his hat, trying to stuff his emotions down his throat, because she looked so much like Marie.

"Morning, John," she replied. "We'd better get going—we have a lot to do today."

He climbed down from the wagon and helped her aboard, holding her soft hand in his rough one, easing her up with his other hand on her waist, and she felt just like Marie.

She settled into her seat, laid the briefcase in the boot. He circled the back of the wagon and climbed beside her, let go the brake, snapped the reins, and they were off.

"Have you been fighting, John?" she asked, peering sideways at him.

"Fell down."

"You know very well you can't get hurt like that by just falling down. Guess you lost the fight."

"No, ma'am."

"You won?"

"A draw."

"What did you fight about?"

"Don't like each other."

"Why not?"

How could he put something that deep and visceral into mere words? "Hard to say."

"You can't even explain what you were fighting about, but it looks as though you've taken a serious beating. Does that make sense, John?"

"No, ma'am."

She sighed in exasperation, and they rode out of the yard, onto the open prairie, heading down the trail to San Antone. Stone glanced at her, sitting next to him in the sunlight, holding her hand over her eyes as she scanned the terrain ahead. Her resemblance to Marie was unearthly. She was Marie and not Marie at the same time.

Stone had taken many buckboard rides with Marie in the old days. They'd find a lonely path, tie the horses to a tree, tear off each other's clothes, and feast upon each other's bodies.

She turned to him, her features serious as a Sunday school teacher describing the Resurrection. "John, I don't want to intrude myself into your life, but you're not like the rest, and you should stop acting like them. You've got to pull yourself together. Do you have any family?"

"No, ma'am."

"Then you'll have to do it yourself, and if you need any help from me, I'll be happy to assist in whatever way I can. You may've forgotten, but you're a gentleman, not riff-raff."

Stone felt as though he were seated beside Marie, although he knew that wasn't so. Marie and Cassandra merged with each other, then separated again before his eyes.

"I'm trying my best," he said.

"A good start would be to swear off fighting. A second would be to stop drinking. I hope you don't plan to indulge while we're in town."

"Can't afford it."

"That's a start. My husband always says if a man wishes to control others, he must first control himself."

"How does *he* do it?"

"Inner strength. Will. His indomitable spirit."

"Must be quite a man."

"The best."

"Maybe if I try hard, I can be like him."

"Maybe you can."

She detected the irony in his voice, but chose not to respond. He puffed his cigarette as he looked ahead at the vast prairie, the long colonnades of mountains trailing toward the horizon, and puffs of cotton-candy clouds floating across the sky. I'll spend the day in church, he thought. A man can't get in trouble in church.

It was a busy day in San Antonio, and the wide main boulevard was crowded with traffic. Stone piloted the horses through the mass of people and animals, and Cassandra looked ahead at the bank, praying the money was deposited in an account she didn't know about, so she could have a good laugh at herself, and then take tea at one of the finer hotels in town, perhaps even have some lunch and a piece of pastry.

Stone looked up at the corner suite of the Barlowe House as he passed by, and wondered if Veronika were there, wearing a black lace nightgown, or maybe nothing at all, lying in bed alone, hoping he'd stop by.

He brought the horses to a stop in front of the bank, climbed down, then helped Cassandra descend to the muck of the street. "I'll meet you in front of the Barlowe House at three o'clock in the afternoon," she said. "Leave the team at the stable, and bill everything to the ranch. Please don't get into any trouble, all right?"

"Yes, ma'am."

"No drinking?"

"Not a drop."

She smiled. "Sobriety is a beautiful thing, John."

"I can see all it's done for your husband."

There it was again, that little dig. She decided not to let this one pass. "Don't you think you're being a little nasty, John?"

"I guess I get you mixed up with my old girlfriend sometimes, ma'am."

"I'm not her, and try to keep that in mind. Also, I don't want you denigrating a man who gave his arm to his country."

Stone lowered his head. "Sorry," he replied.

"You have so much potential," she said, "but you always take the low road. I find that very sad."

She turned abruptly and walked toward the bank. Stone gazed at her outline beneath her dress, then shrugged philosophically, climbed back into the buckboard, rode it into the stable, and unhitched the horses.

Twenty minutes later he was back on the street, wondering what to do with himself. He should go to church and meditate, but somehow that didn't seem like an appropriate place to spend the afternoon in one of the frontier's greatest cities, San Antone.

He decided to wander around and see if anything interesting turned up. Maybe he'd run into an old friend from the past who wouldn't try to kill him, or maybe somebody'd stand him a drink at one of the local saloons.

This might be his last time in town for weeks, maybe months. The cattle drive would be long, with much hardship along the way. He wished he had some money. All he owned worth anything were his guns and Tomahawk, and he couldn't sell either of them.

A crazy idea entered his mind, as his eyes fell on the Barlowe House. Maybe he should visit Veronika, ask her what happened last night, and see if they could resume their little game.

He turned toward the Barlowe House, ran light-footed across the street, feeling clear and good inside, his strength returning, with spring in his muscles and fire in his heart. He slowed down as he approached the Last Chance Saloon.

His mouth watered as he thought of whiskey in a glass sitting on the bar. His hands trembled, and the drinking urge came on him. He wanted to keep walking by the Last Chance Saloon, but somehow his legs wouldn't move in that direction. They were carrying him, almost by themselves, toward the batwing doors.

He pushed them open and entered the saloon, looking around for a familiar face, and his eyes fell on Haliday, sitting alone at a table, staring through half-closed eyes at a half-full glass of whiskey.

Stone pulled up a chair next to him. "How's about a drink, old buddy?"

Haliday stared at him, reached into his pocket, and spilled a handful of coins onto the table. Stone picked up enough to buy a drink of whiskey, and carried the coins to the bar. The bartender placed a glass in front of him, filled it to the line.

Stone sipped the top off the whiskey, then carried the rest to the table, dropping down beside Haliday, who looked at him with disgust. "If'n you hadn't come along last night, everythin'd be all right."

"What you don't realize," Stone replied, "is you're going to Kansas with the Triangle Spur."

"What you don't understand, you crazy son of a bitch, is *I hate cattle*. They're the dumbest creatures God made."

"No dumber than soldiers. Didn't we walk into the slaughter-house too? By the way, is the no-account count in town today?"

"Not that I know of. Why d'ya want to know? Hey—wait a minute—you're not thinkin' . . . !"

Stone winked as he raised his whiskey to his lips. "Why not?"

Mr. Dohenney, president of the Alamo Central Bank, sat at his desk and studied his record through pince-nez glasses. He had a nose like a ferret, and that's what he'd been all his life, looking for the lie in a column of numbers, the deceit in a bank draft, and all the other types of chicanery employed by swindlers, forgers, and embezzlers.

Cassandra sat opposite him, trying to be calm. His office had polished wood walls and heavy drapes over the windows. They might be sitting in a bank office in New Orleans, instead of one on the wild frontier.

Cassandra wasn't comfortable in the world of business, the domain of men. She didn't know much about it, felt inferior to its professional practitioners, and always was certain they were robbing her. But she'd had to enter that world, because she couldn't expect Gideon to deal with these people. That would be too much to ask of a man who'd already given so much to his country.

Mr. Dohenney said, "Here it is—I believe I found it. There are four drafts, twenty-five hundred dollars each, made out to the Sundust Investors Syndicate of Denver, Colorado, signed by the colonel."

"Are you sure?" she asked, leaning forward, wanting to see the proof.

He turned the books around and showed them to her. "These are our official bank records, and I can get confirmation from the Syndicate's bank in Denver, if you like."

She looked at the ledger and saw her husband's name beside the sums of money. "Could someone have forged his hand-writing?"

He smiled indulgently. "We know the colonel here. He comes and goes all the time. Is anything wrong, Mrs. Whiteside?"

"Comes and goes all the time?"

"He frequently writes drafts. But of course you know that. Is there anything else I can do for you, Mrs. Whiteside, because I have rather a lot of work to do, and . . ."

Cassandra found herself on the sidewalk in front of the bank, and thought she was going to pass out. Buildings swam around her, and she reached to a post for support. It had happened, there could be no backing away from it. They were in debt, and might have to sell the ranch, *unless they could get that herd on the trail.*

What had Gideon done, and why? She wanted to return to the ranch immediately, to tell Truscott to take whatever herd he'd formed to Abilene as soon as he could get them moving.

Then, when the creditors came, she could tell them they'd get paid as soon as the herd reached the railhead, but if they came while the herd was there, they'd simply take, on the hoof, what they were owed. *The herd must get moving as soon as possible*.

Where was John Stone? She'd said she'd meet him at three, after the leisurely lunch she'd planned, but now she was sick to her stomach, and it wasn't just the money that did it.

Gideon had lied to her, and that hurt the most. It was almost impossible for her to comprehend, because he was a god to her, and could do no wrong.

Wait a minute, she said to herself, did he ever tell me about this? She wracked her brain and tried to remember the Sundust Syndicate among the many investment ideas he'd discussed with her over the years, but it didn't ring a bell, and she certainly didn't remember authorizing him to invest ten thousand dollars of her inheritance.

Surely there must be a mistake. A man like Gideon couldn't've done such a thing. He was naive when it came to business, so maybe one of his drinking cronies had put him up to it, or used his signature in a fraudulent way. She'd have to discuss it with him immediately.

It was eleven o'clock in the morning, and she had no idea where John Stone was, but suspected the town's innumerable saloons. Perhaps she could hire a boy to look for him, but first she thought her outlook might improve if she had a little brandy.

Holding her skirts in her hands, she crossed the street and climbed the sidewalk on the far side. Then she walked swiftly to the Barlowe House, entered the lobby, and made her way to the restaurant overlooking the street. Perhaps, while she was having refreshments, she could see John Stone pass by.

She sat at a table near one of the front windows, ordered brandy and coffee. The sinking feeling in her stomach wouldn't go away. The Triangle Spur, her great dream, was a bust. How much could she salvage?

Everything would be all right, if she could just get that herd moving to Abilene. Then she'd have a fighting chance, although she'd be depending on the most problematic and useless crew of cowboys ever to go up the trail. She was confident, or wanted to be confident, that Truscott could wring the necessary efficiency out of them.

It occurred to her that in the past she'd often found sums of money missing in her calculations, a hundred here, three hundred there, but she'd always thought it was her erroneous arithmetic. Had Gideon been doing this all along? It was impossible. Unthinkable. She was ashamed for even thinking such a thing.

The waiter placed her brandy and coffee on the table, bowed, and backed away. She hoisted the glass of brandy and drank a good healthy gulp to clear her head. Then she sipped some coffee.

Far down the sidewalk, on the other side of the street, she saw a tall, familiar figure wearing two six-guns in crisscrossed belts. Although she couldn't see his face clearly yet, she knew it was him by his smooth rolling swagger.

She couldn't help smiling, because he really was nothing more than a big brat. Stone needed a momma, or a good strong woman to keep him on the straight and narrow, and then maybe he could make something out of himself.

He crossed the street, heading for the Barlowe House, and she thought maybe he'd heard she was there. She arose and moved toward the lobby, to intercept him, but when she reached the dining-room exit, she saw something that made her stop cold in her tracks.

It was her husband, Colonel Gideon Whiteside, accompanying a young woman across the lobby. Cassandra nearly fell on her face, but caught herself, held tightly, and moved into the shadows. Her husband and the young woman headed toward the front door, and her husband touched his hand to the small of her back, to guide her, just as he did with Cassandra.

Forgotten now was John Stone. What did her husband think he was doing? She ran to her table, tossed down the rest of the brandy, sipped some coffee, threw a few coins on the table, and ran toward the lobby. A few men raised their eyebrows as she passed, and figured she was just another hysterical woman with some petty concern on her little mind.

At the front of the hotel, John Stone climbed the steps to the wide planked veranda, where men and women sat in the open air, sipping beverages, when suddenly he saw, emerging from the lobby, Colonel Whiteside.

Both of them looked at each other, and Stone recognized the young woman on his arm as one of the chorus girls from the Last Chance Saloon.

Stone didn't know what to do, and pretended he hadn't seen Whiteside. He crossed the veranda, passed Whiteside without a murmur, and entered the lobby of the hotel.

Was Whiteside running with a chorus girl behind Cassandra's back? What did women see in that old windbag anyway?

He climbed the stairs, and Cassandra waited until he was out of sight, then moved across the lobby and out onto the sidewalk, turning to her right and left, seeing her husband and the woman, and moving after them, staying in the shadows near the storefronts, her heart beating so furiously she thought she was having a heart attack.

Ahead of her, Rosalie said to Whiteside, "I ain't nothin' to be ashamed of, and there's nothing wrong with you takin' a walk with me. Let me tell you—there's lots of men who wish they was you right now."

"But I'm known in this town," he said. "My wife might find out."

"Who do you love best, Gideon—yer wife or me?"

"You of course, my dear. Didn't I buy you a house? Don't I give you everything you want?"

"You ain't gave me no ring, Gideon. Till then, I'm still a free woman."

"Surely you're not suggesting . . ."

"If you won't marry me, there's plenny who will. Like Mr. Shannon. You know who Mr. Shannon is, don'tcha Gideon? The feller what owns the Bar XT?"

"But Shannon was a war profiteer! Never even put on a uniform in five years of war!"

"The only war I care about, Gideon, is my own war to put food on the table."

"I've bought you a house, but nothing's ever enough. You're insatiable."

"When you sell cattle, you try to get the best price. I got to get my best price too."

Gideon ground his teeth in barely suppressed anger. Somehow he was unable to put this one under his thumb, perhaps because she was even more desperate than he. And he couldn't take the house back; he'd signed it over to her back in the days when they were more cuddly.

It'd been a shock when he'd seen John Stone at the Barlowe House, but Stone hadn't appeared to notice him. Whiteside hoped Stone wouldn't tell Cassandra, because that could cause dangerous complications at a bad time. He'd known he shouldn't walk in broad daylight with Rosalie, but she'd insisted. She had him wrapped around her little finger, because she was beautiful and young, only seventeen, and he was fifty, flabby, and had a double chin.

Cassandra was losing her figure, whereas Rosalie was firm and ripe. Gideon always felt a need for young women, but it was more difficult to get them now that he was fifty.

If a man had sufficient monies, he could have anything he wanted, even Rosalie, and it wouldn't matter if he were ninety. The main thing was gold coins.

It was no use trying to frighten Rosalie into submission. All she had to do was wink and make a casual suggestion to some lovesick drunken cowboys, and Whiteside would be found shot dead on a lonely road, or maybe he'd never be found at all, disappearing unmourned into an unmarked grave on the prairie.

He craved her strong young body, those pert breasts, and couldn't let her go, because if he did it'd mean he was just another foolish old man. Somehow he had to hold on to her.

"The ring will come in due time, my dear," he said, draping his arm over her shoulder. "Haste makes waste. One step at a time."

"What do you mean by *due time*, Gideon? A month? Six months? A year?"

"A year."

"I ain't got a year to wait, Gideon. Sorry."

She wriggled out of his grasp and moved a short distance from him, and it hurt to be spurned on the street where people could see.

"You must give me some time," he begged. "I just can't walk away from my wife. We have to think of her feelings too. I'm in the middle of delicate business negotiations, which I must complete before I can do anything else. But you bear with me a while longer, and have faith in me, and we'll be richer than your wildest dreams. You'll buy whatever you want, and live like a queen."

He saw the greed in her eyes, and knew he'd touched her most significant spot. What she didn't know was his resources always would be limited, even if he ended up with every penny of Cassandra's money. But he could have her for a while, and an old man only needed a while.

"Only three more months?" she asked.

"That's all, and then you can have all the wonderful things you've always wanted, and so richly deserve. Surely you can give me three months, darling. Shannon may have more money than I, but that doesn't mean you'll get any. He's a tight-fisted bastard, with no culture, sensitivity, or ideals." Whiteside balled his fist and held it in front of her face. "He didn't serve in the war! What kind of man could he be?"

"The Bar XT is the second-biggest spread around here, after the Diamond D. Yer spread is just a piddlin' li'l thing, a few thousand cattle. I think you should talk more respectfully about Mr. Shannon, Gideon."

She pointed her nose in the air and increased her pace as she walked swiftly over the planked sidewalk, catching the eyes of cowboys and loafers sitting on the benches, smoking cigarettes and drinking whiskey, admiring the women flesh and talking horseflesh.

Farther back on the sidewalk, Cassandra felt as though she were choking to death. Her husband was rushing to catch up with the young woman, obviously pleading with her. Cassandra had to admit the obvious conclusion: Gideon was passionately involved with her.

Cassandra wanted to catch up with them and ask what was going on, but something held her back. She was afraid it would be too much for her, that close, in all its horror. Better to lag back and observe from a safe distance.

And in fact, she might be misinterpreting everything. There could be an innocent explanation, although it was hard to imagine what one would be.

The cowboys and loafers saw her pass, and a few made admiring comments, then returned to their discussions of horses, because horse traders in San Antone were thick as fiddlers in hell.

John Stone climbed the stairs of the Barlowe House, amazed by what he'd seen. What was Gideon Whiteside doing with one of the dancing girls in Veronika's act? A one-armed old lecher with a woman of shady implications. If Cassandra found out, there'd be hell to pay.

He came to the floor where Veronika lived, and wondered what he'd do if the count opened the door again. Maybe Stone would punch him in the mouth, because it felt like that kind of day.

Stone approached the door, and suddenly it opened. Veronika stepped out, wearing a long dress, carrying a parasol. Their eyes met, and hers clouded over as he came to a stop in front of her.

"I thought we had an appointment," he said.

She looked up at him, and he was only a few inches taller than she. "I knew you vould be trupple the first moment I set eyes on you," she mused. "You are a crazy cowboy, but unfortunately you haf a certain charm." She looked back and forth in the hotel corridor, and no one was about. "I haf someplace to go," she said, "but I can talk for a few minutes."

She unlocked her door, and he followed her into her suite of rooms.

"Haf a seat," she said. "Vould you like something to drink?"

"Whiskey."

"Asking a cowboy if he vants something to drink is like asking a bird if it vants to fly," she replied, walking to a cabinet and pouring a glass of whiskey.

She handed it to him, then sat on a chair, her eyes roving his shoulders and arms, and the dark blond hair on his chest.

"I am sorry about last night," she said, "but the count vas here, undt he, vell, you know how it is."

Stone sipped his whiskey. "I think I do, but he's not here now."

"He is a very jealous man."

"So'm I."

"You haf nothing to be jealous of. You barely know me. Do you think I could afford to live like this if all I did vas shake my ass in the Last Chance Saloon?"

Stone gazed at her over the top of his glass, and felt a powerful eroticism. "I understand all that," he said, "but we're alone now."

"I do not think you understand at all, *schatzchen*. The count is a proud man, and therefore a dangerous one. Yesterday I gave in to a momentary veakness, but now I am myself again. Finish your vhiskey undt leave like a good boy, all right?"

"You sure that's what you want?"

"I vould not tell you if I was not sure."

He saluted her with his glass, then drained its contents and placed the glass on the table beside him. He was about to wipe his mouth with the back of his hand, but remembered his manners. Standing, he adjusted his gunbelts, then headed for the door. She reached it a second before he, her hand touched the doorknob, and he was beside her, only inches away.

The vestibule was narrow and dark, and they looked into each other's eyes. The fragrance of her body arose to his nostrils, and he felt an artery throb in his throat. She saw the flash in his eyes, and could feel his powerful physicality. Her hand faltered on the doorknob, and he swallowed hard. He hadn't touched a woman for more than five years, and here was one of the most stunning he'd ever seen.

"Do not even think about it, *schatzchen,*" she said, but there was a tremulo in her voice.

He placed his hands on her shoulders and drew her closer to him. Their eyes met, and they saw the inferno. Stone thought of Marie, Cassandra, and every other woman he'd ever desired, and somehow they all accumulated in the woman before him, whose body was melting into his.

He held her tightly against him, felt her heart beating, and a gigantic dam burst inside him. She dug her fingernails into his back, and he pressed his lips against hers, as together they sank toward the floor.

Colonel Whiteside and Rosalie Cowper stopped at a neat two-storied house at the edge of town. Whiteside opened the white picket gate, and together they proceeded up the path toward the front door. She opened the door with her key, he bowed and held out his hand, and she went in first.

Cassandra stared at the house from an alley farther down the street, and thought her mind would go into convulsions. This was her second major blow of the day, and she responded in the same way, she reached out for support.

Fortunately the side of a building was there, and it prevented her from falling. Her husband, who'd been a god to her, had become an untrustworthy and sneaky scoundrel.

For a few moments she didn't know where she was. She thought of New Orleans, where she'd been a girl, so happy before the war. Life had seemed golden and radiant, and somehow this had happened. It seemed like a cruel joke perpetrated by a demon.

"Are you all right, lady?"

It was a boy of ten, dressed like a miniature cowboy, his face freckled, looking up at her.

"Yes, thank you," she replied, trying to make a little smile.

She walked back toward the Barlowe House, dragging her feet. *Maybe I'm jumping to conclusions*, she thought. *Everything might be quite innocent, and this only an attack of jealousy unsupported by fact, but it sure doesn't seem that way.*

One part of her wanted to go to the house and get some answers, and another told her to wait and question Gideon next time she saw him. In the meanwhile, maybe she could find out who owned that house.

She headed toward City Hall, and the men sitting on benches admired her slim waist, firm bosom, and bright golden hair.

"You know," an old sourdough said, leaning drunkenly against a wall, "that one's enuff to make a feller think about settlin' down and havin' kids."

"You're too old to have kids—you old varmint," a young cowboy replied, a bottle of potent amber liquid in his hand.

"But I could try," the sourdough told him, his eyes glassy as he stared at the figure of Cassandra receding into the traffic of the lazy San Antonio afternoon.

On the third floor of the Barlowe House, Stone buttoned his jeans while Veronika tied a black silk robe around her waist, the nipples of her breasts pressing against the thin material. Stone walked to the mirror and turned around, to take a look at his back.

It was crisscrossed with deep scratches from her long finger-nails. The blood had dried now, and it looked like brown ink.

"I am very sorry about that, *schatzchen*," she said. "Some-times I go crazy vhen I make love. I cannot help myself. I vill kiss it better."

She came behind him and touched her lips to his back. He turned around, and they embraced. She looked into his eyes. "You look sad," she said. "I hope you do not feel bad about anything."

"The only thing I feel bad about is I don't want to leave. Isn't there some way I can stay for a while?"

"I do not think so, *schatzchen*. You are just a poor cowboy, and it vould never vork."

"We could get along all right, with the both of us work-ing."

"I do not vant to get along *all right*. I vant to get along *vell*. Undt besides, you vill only leave me someday, because all the others haf, undt you are no different from any other man, except in one particular area, vhere you are quite excellent, by the way. I like you very much, undt if you were as vealthy as the count, I vould probably fall in love vith you, but since you are not, there is nothing to fall in love vith. The count is a jealous man, as I told you before, and he vould not hesitate to kill you, so I think you had better leave."

"I'm not easy to kill," he said, pulling her closer to him.

She pressed the tips of her fingers against his chest, and pushed him away. "Do not get any ideas," she said. "It did not mean anything at all."

"That's not true." He reached for her again, because it felt so good to touch a woman after such a long time.

"You must not make it more than it was, *schatzchen*. Please go now. Do not start trouble for me."

Stone was a southern gentleman, and would only push so far. "Maybe we'll run into each other someday," he said, stepping back.

"That vould be lovely, but please put on your boots."

He sat on a chair and reached for his socks, as she lit a cigarette and watched him. He pulled on his boots, donned his shirt, and strapped on his matched Colts. Then he picked up his hat and held it in his hands.

"I'll never forget you," he said.

"That is what the cowboys say to all the girls," she replied. "Good-bye, Johnny. Try to stay out of trupple."

Stone pecked her lips, then moved into the hall, putting on his old Confederate cavalry hat, tilting it to a rakish angle. "If you ever want something money can't buy, just call my name, and I'll be there."

He winked, touched his finger to the brim of his hat, and strolled down the hall toward the stairs.

"What can I do for you, Mrs. Whiteside?" asked the elderly lady behind the desk.

"I'm interested in purchasing a certain piece of property, and I'd like to know who owns it." She told the clerk the address.

"Of course, Mrs. Whiteside."

The old lady, who wore a green eyeshade, pulled down a big book, laid it on the desk, and flipped through the pages. "Here it is," she said. "That property belongs to Miss Rosalie Cowper."

"Who's she?"

"One of the dancers at the Last Chance Saloon." The old lady raised one of her brows, revealing her bleary rheumy eyeball.

"When did she buy the property?" Cassandra asked.

"About a month ago. Oh, my goodness!"

The old lady stared at the book, an expression of surprise on her face.

"What's wrong?" Cassandra asked.

"It says here that she bought the property from your husband!"

Cassandra felt a dagger pierce her heart. "How much was the property?" Cassandra asked.

"Ten thousand dollars."

For the third time that day, Cassandra nearly collapsed. She reached to the desk for support.

"Is anything wrong, Mrs. Whiteside?

"Haven't been feeling well lately."

"Maybe you should see Dr. Linden."

Cassandra walked out of City Hall. Weathered wooden benches leaned against the wall, and a group of cowboys sat on them. She lowered herself onto an empty spot, and tried to assimilate what was happening. It was like a nightmare where circumstances kept going from bad to worse, while her terror mounted.

She felt as though her world had been torn apart, and didn't know what was real. Gideon was stealing her money and giving it to a dancing girl? It was the kind of thing a cowboy might do, but not a man like her husband. He was one of the Confederacy's great heroes, he'd left his arm at Sharpsburg, it was impossible.

The written record didn't lie. She was confused, in pain, with tears streaming down her cheeks. She had no close friends, her husband was her life, and she had nowhere to turn.

The unmistakable aroma of cow manure arose to her nostrils. She saw a filth-encrusted handkerchief hanging in front of her face, held by the cowboy sitting beside her. It was splattered with a suspicious substance, and a dead beetle was entwined in its shrouds. The odor suggested that the cowboy had used it to wipe off his boots.

"No thank you," she said.

"It always hurts to see a lady cry," the cowboy said, and it looked as though he were on the verge of tears himself.

Cassandra couldn't help smiling. "Thank you anyway," she replied, rising to her feet, "and if you're looking for a job, I'm hiring at the Triangle Spur."

"You the boss lady of the Triangle Spur?" the cowboy asked.

"That's right."

"Now I know why you're cryin'!"

The other cowboys guffawed, and Cassandra felt offended. "What's wrong with the Triangle Spur?" she asked.

"Waal," the cowboy drawled out the side of his mouth, "they say the Triangle Spur has got the most stove-up cowboys in Texas."

"That's not true!" Cassandra said indignantly. "They're as fine a bunch of men who ever rode the range!"

The cowboys burst into laughter, holding their sides. Cassandra walked toward the Barlowe House, and the big brass clock suspended from the front of the bank said it was nearly one o'clock in the afternoon. She was anxious to return to the ranch, because no matter what her husband was doing, she had to get the herd moving.

She looked back and forth, hoping to see John Stone, but he wasn't visible on the crowded sidewalks. She decided to return to the Barlowe House and have lunch at one of the window tables, where she might see him on the sidewalk.

I'm going to stay calm, she said to herself as she crossed the street. I'm going to get through this somehow.

Stone sat in a corner of the Last Chance Saloon, sipping a glass of whiskey, and he hadn't felt this relaxed in years. It was as though a thousand tiny anxieties had evaporated in Veronika's arms.

It had been totally insane for a while there, more like two tigers coupling in the mountains than two human beings. His back was ripped to shreds, and he had sucker bites all over his body.

Now he realized what he'd given up during the years he searched for Marie, and it had been his essential manhood, he'd snuffed the life out of it, for Marie's sake.

What if Marie still were alive, and what if he saw her again someday? How could he tell her? Well, maybe she'd have a lot to tell him too. They'd tell each other, have a laugh, and go to bed.

Marie had been subtle, able to drive him wild with a sigh, or a sly little movement, whereas Veronika had nearly broken him into pieces. Her mouth had been ambrosia, her breasts ripe fruit. No longer did he want to punch a stranger in the mouth. It was all gone, and he realized how unhealthy it'd been, to be without the love of women for so long.

He looked around the saloon, and it was the usual afternoon crowd of cowpokes, gamblers, Mexican vaqueros, and ladies who'd do anything for a price. He wished he could've spent the afternoon with Veronika.

He wanted to go back to her, because he wasn't nearly finished. There were lots of things he wanted to do, and was sure she'd be willing. They didn't get much wilder than Veronika. But he'd probably never see her again, because of the count. She'd rather be a rich man's darling than a poor man's slave.

He looked around the saloon at the sporting ladies, and didn't want to pay for it. He'd feel degraded, couldn't do it, so he'd have to find someone else, but what woman in her right mind wanted a poor wandering cowboy?

If he were a rancher, with his own spread, then he could have any woman he wanted. Somehow he had to learn the cattle business, but that's what he was doing. He was going up the trail with the Triangle Spur, and that should teach him what he needed to know. He'd save his money and build a little camp, hire a few cowboys, and brand mavericks. Many a herd had started in just that manner.

He wondered what brand he'd use. Maybe the Bar JS, for his initials? He dreamed of his own herd, his ranch house in the middle of the prairie, and a good woman at his side, but somehow her face was indistinct.

"I thought you'd be in here!" said Cassandra Whiteside.

He raised his eyes, and for a moment felt a stab of remorse for what he'd done with Veronika, but then realized it was Cassandra Whiteside, his employer.

He jumped to his feet. "Yes, ma'am."

"I asked the waiter at the Barlowe House what the most lowdown, filthy saloon in town was, and he said this one. I thought you'd be here."

"Weren't we supposed to meet at three?"

"Something's happened. I'll tell you on the way back to the ranch."

"Can I finish my whiskey?"

"Oh, God—go ahead!"

He downed it, wiped his mouth with the back of his hand, and followed her out of the Last Chance Saloon.

"May I see you tomorrow?" asked Gideon Whiteside, standing in the vestibule of the home he'd bought for Miss Rosalie Cowper.

"I'll be busy," she replied. "Sorry."

His coat was on, and he was ready to leave, but he said, "Busy doing what?"

"Goin' shoppin' with a friend of mine. Care to come along?"

"No thank you," he replied, because her shopping trips were always hazardous to his wallet. "But I hope you're not seeing another man behind my back, are you?"

"I'm a one-man woman," she replied. "You got three months to git that money, so's we can git hitched. After that, I ain't promisin' nothin', Gideon."

"I understand, darling. Now give me a kiss and I'll be on my way."

She pursed her lips, and he touched them with his, pressing his body against hers, feeling her firm young breasts, becoming intoxicated.

She opened the door. "Nice seein' you again, Gideon. There's nobody I'd rather take a bath with than good old Gideon."

He raised his finger to his lips. "Ssshhhh. . . ." he said, turning and walking away.

He placed his hat on his head, tapped it down, and headed for the center of town, a spring in his step that hadn't been there before. That was the effect she had on him. He felt young and sleek again, capable of anything, instead of the graying wreck he saw in the mirror every morning.

Somehow he had to get his hands on a large sum of money, so he could stay with her longer, and there was only one thing to do: sell the herd to Count Von Falkenheim at the Diamond D or Shannon at the Bar XT.

He didn't think there'd be any trouble. Everybody thought he held the purse strings of the Triangle Spur, and Cassandra played along with it. He'd take the money and run with Rosalie, maybe to St. Louis or some other big city where he could find a rich new wife.

It was getting more difficult all the time, and he'd probably have to settle for an old lady next time, with pouches under her eyes and varicose veins. It was too horrible to contemplate, but it was the only way to get money without working, and there wasn't much work for a one-armed man who thought everything beneath him.

He glanced into the street, and was startled to see his wife and John Stone in the buckboard, heading his way. He ducked into the nearest alley and stood in the shadows, peering at them. It looked as though they were engaged in serious discussion, as their wagon passed through the traffic in the middle of the wide boulevard.

He waited until they were gone, then slipped out of the alley and headed toward the stable, to get his horse. He intended to visit Von Falkenheim at the Diamond D, and begin negotiations for sale of the herd.

He thought of lying in the tub with Rosalie, while she did all those wicked things, and quickened his pace, because the sooner he sold the herd, the sooner he'd be back in the tub with her.

Cassandra never did wicked things. She was a lady, and far too proper. But Rosalie was a dancing girl, and she'd do anything.

The cowboys and loafers watched Whiteside walking swiftly over the sidewalk, swinging his arm vigorously through the air, on his way to the Diamond D, to sell his wife down the river.

"Now let me get this straight," Stone said as the wagon rocked over the trail. "If we don't move the herd out tomorrow morning, you're wiped out completely?"

"I'm afraid that's so," she said.

"Don't know much about cattle, but didn't think they could be moved that fast."

"I'll have to talk with Truscott as soon as I return. He'll do it for me. He's the finest foreman in Texas."

"I've never seen him sober."

"The man knows his cattle."

Stone turned sideways and looked at her. "Why do we have to leave so quickly?"

"A large sum of money is missing, and drafts have been written against it. When the holders of those drafts can't get paid, they'll take the cattle. That's why I've got to get the herd out of here, otherwise I'm ruined, and you might see me in a saloon someday, selling what those other girls sell."

"I'd never let that happen to you."

She laughed darkly. "What could you do?"

Stone made a fist and flexed his arm. "I've got this, and with it I could take care of you and me until you got on your feet."

She looked at him, and was touched. "But you don't even know me."

"I know you well enough. As long as I'm around, you'll never have to sell yourself in the Last Chance Saloon."

"I think I'm going to cry."

She pulled her handkerchief out of her sleeve and sobbed softly. This was the cry she wanted to have when she'd been in town, but she hadn't wanted anybody to see her. Now she could let go, and Stone placed his arm around her shoulders.

"Don't worry," he said. "They'll have to fight the bunkhouse to get that herd, and I for one would hate to go against that bunch. They're one mean crew of cowboys."

"But we don't have enough of them for the drive. Last time I spoke with Truscott, he needed at least five more."

"We'll make it—don't you worry. But what's the rush? What happened to your money?"

"Somebody spent it, but . . . ah . . . that's personal, and I don't think I should discuss it with you."

"I know who spent it," Stone said. "You don't have to say a word."

A tear rolled down her cheek, and then she sobbed. His arm still was around her shoulder, and he hugged her tightly, to give her strength.

"I can't believe he'd do this to me," she said, pain and hurt in her voice.

Tears rolled down her cheeks, and she sobbed uncontrollably as the betrayal sank deeper and deeper into her soul.

7

ATOP HIS PRANCHING horse, Gideon Whiteside admired the Diamond D's huge main residence, constructed like an imperial Prussian hunting lodge, with chalet windows and a steep gabled roof, incongruous among the barns and other outbuildings nearby.

Everything was freshly painted and in good repair, unlike the Triangle Spur, where everything was falling apart. Whiteside looked at the cowboys, and they were a hardy bunch, unlike the physical wrecks and misfits at the Triangle Spur. *No wonder nobody respects me*, Whiteside thought. *I own a second-rate spread, but not for long.*

He dismounted in front of the main house, tied his horse to the rail, and marched stalwartly toward the front door, knocking on it with his fist.

The door was opened by a middle-aged man in a butler's uniform. "Yes?"

"I'd like to see the count, if you don't mind."

"Who shall I say is calling, sir?" the butler asked in a German accent.

"Colonel Whiteside."

"Please haf a seat, Colonel. I vill see if the count is available."

Whiteside dropped into the nearest chair and looked at paintings of well-dressed men and women, and the landscapes of

Prussia interspersed with mounted heads of buffalo, antelope, wild pig, and mountain sheep. There was a huge fireplace made out of boulders, and a suit of armor in a corner, standing like a sentinel.

This is what real money can do, Whiteside thought, realizing he must, for the sake of comfort, start marrying wealthier women.

He'd thought Cassandra was wealthy, but it turned out she didn't have that much. He'd found her in the nick of time, though. He'd been penniless, nearly reduced to begging, when she'd come along. She was a patriotic girl, thank God, but she was too nice, and a little too old; he preferred slutty teenagers for companionship.

The butler returned and bowed. "Vould you come vith me, please?"

Whiteside arose and followed him up a flight of stairs, to a wide veranda facing the open prairie. At the edge of the veranda, standing at an easel, was Count Von Falkenheim, a paintbrush in his hand. Beside him was a table with pots of paint, and he was dressed in the style of a Prussian nobleman, with tight pants and billowing shirtsleeves.

"I didn't know you painted," Whiteside said, gazing at the landscape on the canvas. "It's quite good, but personally, I prefer battle scenes that show the glory of . . ."

"Vhat do you vant!" the count said sharply, interrupting him.

"Well . . . I . . ."

The count shot a cold glance at him, then dabbed a white cloud onto the blue sky. He appeared annoyed, and that made Whiteside more nervous.

"I was wondering," Whiteside managed to get out, "whether you'd be interested in buying my ranch, including the herd."

"How much?"

"How does twenty-five thousand dollars sound?"

The count looked at him with haughty repugnance. "Do not be idiotic. Your cattle are worth little in Texas, and your ranch property is a joke. But vhy do you want to sell, Vhiteside? I thought you vere sending your herd to Kansas. That is vhere to get your price."

"I need the money now."

The count wrinkled his brow, lay down his paintbrush, and swaggered toward Whiteside, examining his features as if a secret lay hidden within them.

"I vill offer ten thousand dollars," he said.

Whiteside smiled. "Now you're idiotic."

"Am I? Vell, if you think so, leave."

The count returned to his canvas and resumed painting, putting green on the grass of the prairie. It was as if Whiteside had ceased to exist, and Whiteside became perturbed. The man wasn't even an American, and was treating him like dirt.

"Personally," said Whiteside, "I don't know why they let people like you into this country. You don't know how to behave."

The count raised his courtly eyebrows and chuckled. "They let every lowlife and criminal into this country, so vhy should they not let me in? I mean, they even let *you* in."

"I was born here, sir," Whiteside said proudly. "This is my country. I have given my blood for it, and now here I am insulted by a man who knows nothing of our proud traditions, and in fact doesn't care about them at all."

The count looked at Whiteside, then threw his paintbrush in a bowl. "Haf a seat," he said. "Vould you like something to drink?"

"Whiskey, if you please."

The count wiped his hands, then pulled a sash. A few moments later the butler arrived, and the count whispered something into his ear. Then the count sat on a chair opposite Whiteside, and Whiteside thought he'd taught the count a lesson about America. He was sure the count would treat him with greater respect in the future, because he'd stood up to him, and showed he couldn't be pushed around.

The count rested his ankle upon his knee, and he wore highly polished Prussian officer's boots. "I belief you know I vas a soldier, and I too fought in a var. It vas not a big var, but it was a var, and I saw my share of blood.

"I served on the staff of Field Marshal Helmuth Karl Bernhard Graf von Moltke, whom most Americans haf never heard of, but he was a great man, in the same class, I vould say, as your Generals Lee and Grant. One day I heard him say that most battles are von before the first shot is fired, because preparation is everything.

"Although I manage this ranch, I am still essentially a soldier, and I see all life as var. Therefore, when I came to this area, I made certain I had sufficient supplies, I made certain my location was correct, and I made it my business to find out everything about the people I vould be dealing vith. Haf you ever heard of the Pinkerton Agency."

"Pinkerton was a spy for the Yankees," said Whiteside derisively.

"Undt a very good one. I hired the Pinkertons to investigate every person of consequence in this region."

The count gazed coolly at Whiteside, and Whiteside went pale. The butler entered with two glasses of whiskey, a bottle, and a folder. He served the whiskey and handed the folder to the count.

"Drink up," the count said to Whiteside. "You are going to need it."

Whiteside raised the glass to his lips, and his hand was trembling. The count sipped his whiskey, then opened the folder.

"Your real name is George Valmsley and you vere born in New York City, in 1820, the son of an actress, father unknown. Your mother traveled frequently, taking you vith her, undt your career on the stage began vhen you vere four. You vere first arrested at the age of ten for picking pockets. You vere arrested again at the age of twelve for petty thievery."

"You don't have to read that," Whiteside said in a shaking voice.

"Oh, but I do, my dear *colonel*. After all, you told me I am not fit to be in this country, because I did not shed my blood for it, undt I feel compelled to introduce you to several facts. Please permit me to continue. After getting out of prison, you moved to Philadelphia and secured a position in a bank, but then, at the age of twenty-two, you vere arrested for embezzling bank funds, undt vent to prison again."

"I've heard enough of this," Whiteside said, getting to his feet.

"Sit down," the count said in a deadly voice.

"I'm afraid I'm not feeling well."

"You are going to feel a lot vorse if you do not sit down."

Whiteside didn't know what to do. Bending his knees, he dropped heavily into the chair.

"Then it appears you began your career of marrying vomen for their money, sucking them dry, undt leaving them. A few of your vives have died under mysterious circumstances, but no one has ever been able to charge you vith murder. Then the var came, your name was called for conscription, so you fled south to Virginia, but then the Confederacy drafted you. You deserted them too. They caught you undt put you in prison, but you promised to be a good soldier in the future, undt they released you. You were sent to Sharpsburg, but deserted again, undt vhile fleeing the battlefield, you vere vounded by cannon.

"Since the war, you haf played the part of wounded hero, knowing full well that most people never check the facts. But I do, because I served under Field Marshal von Moltke, undt learned my lessons well." The count folded the dossier, placed it on the table beside him, and drank some whiskey.

Whiteside's back had been to the wall many times in his life, and he was completely calm, calculating his chances. "What are you going to do?" he asked.

"I am not going to do anything," the count replied. "Your life has no significance to me at all. I just vanted you to know that you must not play var hero vith me, because I am not a fool like everyone else around here."

Whiteside finished off his whiskey and placed the glass on the table beside him. "My cattle are still for sale."

"Your cattle? But they are your vife's cattle, no? Her money bought them, am I wrong?"

"Under the laws of this country, my wife's property is my property, and I'm legally entitled to sell it. You offered me ten thousand dollars, and I accept. If you have the money here, we can transact the business right now."

"Not so fast," the count said. "How do I know how many cattle you haf, and vhat their condition is? I must see vhat I am buying."

"My cattle are in San Jacinto Valley, if you want to examine them."

"I know vhere they are," the count replied. "I even know vhere Rosalie Cowper is."

Whiteside's face turned red. "Now just a minute!"

The count smiled. "You are an utter scoundrel, but I think maybe ve can do business, Vhiteside, or should I call you Valmsley? Vith a man like you, it is hard to know." The count threw back his head and laughed.

Stone steered the wagon into the yard of the Triangle Spur, and Cassandra jumped to the ground before the wheels stopped turning. She ran to the bunkhouse, flung open the door, and saw Slipchuck nailing the table together, because it had broken down during lunch.

"Do you know where Truscott is!" Cassandra asked, gazing in amazement at the spindly old man in front of her. How could this man possible survive a cattle drive?

Slipchuck knew he was talking to the boss lady, and drew himself to attention. "He's thataway!" he replied, pointing vaguely in a southwesterly direction.

"How far?"

"An hour's ride."

"Tell him I must speak with him as soon as possible."

"But he told me to stay behind and . . ."

Slipchuck cut off the sentence in midair, because her eyes were absolutely ferocious. "Yes, ma'am," he said.

He turned and ran out the door with a vitality that surprised her, like a young boy in an old man's body. Maybe he'll make it after all, she thought whimsically, as she looked around the bunkhouse.

She'd never been here before, and it reeked with tobacco smoke and the odor of stale whiskey. The floor hadn't been swept for weeks, maybe months, and had leaves and pinecones upon it. The cuspidor was overflowing in the corner. No beds were made, and pictures of naked women were nailed to the walls. Filthy clothes were strewn everywhere. How can they live like this?

A figure moved in the shadows, and she became frightened. "Who's there?"

Ephraim stepped forward, shuffling his feet. "Jus' me, ma'am."

"You're the cook, aren't you?"

"Yes, ma'am."

"I hear you're very good."

He clasped his hands together and bent slightly. "Yes, ma'am. I tries my best."

"Where's your kitchen?"

"This way, ma'am."

He led her into the shadows, through a passageway, and then into a medium-sized room with a big black stove in the corner. The room was immaculately clean, and the aroma from the pots was heavenly.

"What are you cooking?"

"Beef stew. Care to try some?"

She watched as he ladled stew into a tin bowl, and thought him a fine example of his race, with his high cheekbones, beautiful brown eyes, and a physique that reminded her of John Stone, but he'd been in a fight recently, and his face was badly bruised.

He handed her the bowl, and she spooned some up. It tasted better than it smelled, and that was saying something. "Where did you learn to cook?" she asked.

"My momma taught me."

"She taught you well. Where is she now."

"She's dead."

"I'm sorry to hear that, but at least she gave you something to remember her by."

"That's so," he replied. "It's as if she's still feedin' me."

"Did you hear me speaking with that old man a little while ago?"

"That's ole Slipchuck, ma'am, and yes, I did hear."

"I sent him for Truscott, because we're taking the herd up the trail immediately. How soon can you have the chuck wagon ready to roll?"

"I'd have to go to town fo' supplies, and then it'll take a few hours to load the wagon and hitch the horses."

Cassandra realized it was impossible to get the herd moving in the morning, but maybe the next morning. Yes, the next morning.

"I want you in town when the store opens in the morning, and charge everything to my account."

"Somebody will have to come wif me. You see, ma'am, a darky like me can't buy all that stuff unless a white man is along to vouch fo' me."

"Pick anybody you want, and tell him it was my orders."

Suddenly it hit her. She'd have to leave the ranch too, otherwise her creditors would find her, and maybe they could put her in jail! She'd have to go into hiding, or *go up the trail!*

"You all right, ma'am."

It was the best all-round solution, and when they reached Kansas, she'd ride ahead and make arrangements to sell the herd in Abilene. Then she could pay off her creditors, and hopefully she'd have enough left to start another venture.

"I'm fine," she said to Ephraim. "Well, it's been nice meeting you. I'm sure we'll be seeing a lot of each other from now on."

She turned and walked out of the kitchen, passing through the main room of the bunkhouse, and the stench was incredible. She couldn't understand how Truscott permitted it, but evidently he didn't care how the men lived, as long as they did their work.

She didn't see it the same way. Hereafter she'd supervise the men more carefully. They obviously had little self-respect. She couldn't let them live like this.

She crossed the yard, heading for the main house, as the sun dropped behind the horizon, shooting rays into the sky. She felt better, as if she were fighting back, and she'd get the herd to Abilene even if she had to work side by side with the men.

She entered the main house, climbed the stairs to her room, and dropped into the chair beside her bed, looking at the tip of the sun as it sank below the horizon. The sky went green for a split second, and then was suffused with a bright red glow.

She pulled off her boots and leaned back in her chair, closing her eyes. A faint perspiration was on her forehead and cheeks, and her eyelashes were curled like tiny scimitars.

There was nothing more to do, and she was free to relax, think, and test her capacity to handle the pain.

Evidently Gideon had taken ten thousand dollars of her money, and bought that dancing girl a house. No one ever had betrayed her before, and it was a bitter pill.

She couldn't imagine how anybody could be so cruel. Her mother had told her to beware of men, but she thought she could trust Colonel Gideon Whiteside.

Of course, she'd never known much about him. He'd been friendly with a group of other ex-officers, and she assumed he was like them, men of honor who'd given everything they had for the Cause. People from the better class of society certainly had respected Gideon in New Orleans.

She began to doubt her perceptions. Maybe she was passing too hasty a judgment on him. Perhaps there was a reasonable explanation, although it was hard to imagine what one was.

She'd give him a chance to explain, and reserve judgment until then. Yes, that was the proper way. A person was supposed to be innocent until proven guilty.

She arose and unzipped her dress, stepping out of it and putting on a comfortable cotton frock without a flounce or lace on the collar. She had work to do, because she was going up the trail to Kansas. She'd heard of other women who'd done it, and if they could, by God so could she.

She ran down the stairs to the kitchen, and saw Agnes, her maid, putting up vegetables in jars.

"Agnes," Cassandra said, "I'm afraid there's been a change in plans. We're moving the herd out day after tomorrow, and I'm going too. You can come along with us, but if you don't, I'm afraid tomorrow will be your last day."

Agnes was forty-eight years old, with short, straight graying black hair, and a grin came over her rawboned, hard-working country-woman features. "You'd take me with you, ma'am?"

"If you don't mind waiting until Abilene for your pay."

"I been hearin' cowboys talkin' about going up the trail so much it's been comin' out of my ears, and I always wanted to know what it'd be like myself."

"Here's your chance," Cassandra replied.

"How will you and Colonel Whiteside be travelin', ma'am?"

Cassandra looked away. "I don't think Colonel Whiteside will be coming with us."

Tomahawk stood at the edge of the corral, watching Stone approach, his hat low over his eyes, his guns hung low, and a certain looseness in his gait that Tomahawk had never seen before.

"Hello, Tomahawk," Stone said, patting him on the mane. "What's been going on?"

Tomahawk smelled the woman on his shirt, and noticed the gentleness of his touch.

"Taking good care of you?"

Stone walked around Tomahawk, looking him over, making sure there were no sores or other signs of trouble, tapped him on the rear left hoof. Tomahawk craned his neck around and looked at him with his huge eyes.

"We're going to Kansas pretty soon," Stone said. "It's going to be a hell of a trip, but you take care of me, and I'll take care of you. Is it a deal?"

Tomahawk whinnied, and Stone stepped back. It was as if the animal understood what he said, but that was impossible.

"Rest as much as you can, because it's going to be rough until we get to Abilene. See you in the morning."

Stone turned and walked away, and Tomahawk shook his head from side to side. Then he turned and looked at the other horses in the corral. They were milling about, with nothing to do until one of the cowboys had someplace to go, and then it was off with no notion of where you were going.

Tomahawk had been owned by cowboys who'd mistreated him, and it had been a harsh life. But the new boss never mistreated him, although he was awfully forgetful. Maybe now, after the woman, he wouldn't forget so much.

Tomahawk raised his head and saw a palomino mare across the dust of the corral. She held her head high, her eyes bright, and she looked directly at him. He bowed his head and moved toward her.

It was dark when Duke Truscott climbed off his horse in front of Cassandra's house. He was dusty, his ass hurt, and he wondered what the the boss lady wanted.

He didn't like to deal with her, because she didn't know a goddamn thing about ranching. Neither did her husband, but at least he was a man. Women could drive a man crazy.

He knocked on the door, and it was opened by Agnes, with whom he was on friendly terms.

"What does she want?" Truscott asked, removing his hat.

"I think I'd better let her tell you, Ramrod. Take a load off yer feet, and how's about some lemonade?"

"If you can pour a little whiskey into it, Miss Agnes, I'd be grateful."

She walked away, and he sat on one of the chairs. He'd been cutting cattle all day, and was exhausted. But the herd was coming together. Should be able to move out in about another week.

Cassandra walked into the room, a big smile on her face, and Agnes was a few feet behind her, the glass of spiked lemonade on her tray, and she also was smiling. *What the hell's goin' on here?* Truscott wondered as he rose to his feet.

"You wanted to see me, ma'am?"

"Be seated, Mr. Truscott, and drink your lemonade."

Truscott felt like a steer being sent to slaughter as he picked the glass of lemonade off the tray. Cassandra sat opposite him and crossed her legs, gazing at him, trying to measure the man.

She knew he didn't want to have anything to do with her, but somehow she had to get him to do what she wanted. "There's been a change in plans," Cassandra told him, "due to a severe emergency. Today is Tuesday, and I'm afraid we have to put the herd on the trail first thing Thursday morning. I know it won't be easy, but it's an absolute necessity."

She paused to let him speak, and he stared at her incredulously, thinking that all women were insane, but he couldn't tell her that, because she was the boss lady.

"Ma'am," he said stiffly, "it just plain can't be done."

"I understand that," she replied. "An ordinary ramrod could never work under that kind of pressure, but you're different, Truscott, and you know it. You know more about cattle than anyone else in the world, and the men'll do anything you say. You can do it—I know you can."

Truscott raised his right palm. "You don't realize what it takes to form a herd, ma'am. Yer cattle is scattered all over the county."

"I thought you've been rounding them up."

"We don't have 'em yet by a long shot."

"How many do you have?"

"Around two thousand head."

"We'll leave with them, and whatever else you can gather tomorrow."

"But, ma'am, you're throwin' away nearly half yer herd!"

"Two fifths, to be exact, and I know it, and I don't like it, but you see, Mr. Truscott, if I don't get that herd moving, I'll be in serious financial difficulties, and I may not be able to pay your back wages."

Truscott shrugged. "Could take my wages in cattle."

"That's true, and I'll tell everybody you left me in the lurch, and you'll see whether you ever work as a foreman again. But I'd hope it wouldn't come to that, Mr. Truscott. I'd hope you'd follow orders, as the ramrod of the Triangle Spur."

"What does yer husband say?"

"He has nothing to do with this. This is my ranch, bought with his money. Who hands you your wages at the end of every month? I'm in charge here, and I've given you your instructions. Are you or aren't you going to follow them?"

Truscott finished off his glass of lemonade, and a tray appeared magically in front of him, in Agnes's hands. He placed the glass onto it, and Agnes said, "Why don't you stop bein' a hardass, Truscott, and do what you're told like all the rest of us around here?"

Truscott had known he was defeated when he saw both of them coming at him with lemonade. "I'll do my best," he grumbled, reaching for his hat. "Might as well git started right now."

He arose and walked out of the living room. Cassandra and Agnes waited until he closed the door behind him, and then embraced triumphantly in the middle of the dining-room floor.

"The man ain't never been borned," Agnes said, "who can stand up to *two* determined women and some good old-fashioned lemonade!"

Truscott walked into the bunkhouse and saw four men gathered around the table, playing cards in the light of the lamp, and the rest of the cowboys in bed.

"Everybody up!" he hollered, whacking sleeping men over their heads with his leather gloves. "Let's hit it—you sons of bitches!"

Stone was in a deep sleep when the gloves smacked his ear. He opened his eyes and rolled over to see what the commotion was about.

"Drop yer cocks and grab yer socks!" Truscott roared, pulling the *segundo* out of his bed by his hair, and the dog, who was wrapped in the *segundo's* arms, yelped and kicked his legs, trying to escape from the dreaded ramrod of the Triangle Spur.

"On yer feet!"

Stone climbed down from his bunk, wearing only his underwear, and it reminded him of West Point, the surprise inspections in the middle of the night, but this was a bunkhouse that hadn't been cleaned for many months, maybe even years, whereas the barracks at West Point had been spotless, and you could eat off the floor, should that ever become necessary.

The cowboys moved toward the open area near the table, and surrounded Truscott, who wore his old banged-up range hat with the high crown covered with dents and rain stains.

"Tomorrow we git up two hours early!" Truscott told them. "We got to form the herd, because we're goin' up the trail first thing on Thursday morning!"

"Ain't enough time!" the *segundo* protested, a surprised look on his face.

"I just gave you yer orders!" Truscott replied. "Ephraim— check the chuck wagon, and if it needs any work, ask the *segundo* to assign somebody to do it! The rest of us'll ride to San Jacinto Valley to form up the herd! Are there any questions!"

Blakemore raised his hand.

Truscott scowled at him. "I kinda thought the Yankee would open his big mouth. What is it now, Blakemore?"

"I was wonderin' if we could have time to go to town and have our last good time, because Abilene is a long ways off."

"You're sayin' you want to git drunk? Is that what I'm hearin', Blakemore? Well tell me this. After we form up the herd, who's gonna keep it together if all you cowboys go into town to get drunk?"

"Can't the cattle just stay by themselves for the night?"

Truscott gazed at him for several seconds with an expression of supreme distaste, then stepped toward the door and said,

"From now on, nobody goes to town without my permission! Git some sleep, cowboys—this might be yer last chance till we hit Abilene!"

Truscott slammed the door behind him, and the men looked at each other.

"Goddamn son of a bitch bastard whoremaster!" the *segundo* said, driving his fist into the wall.

The cabin shook, and the men grumbled as they returned to their bunks. They'd thought they'd have one last night on the town. But their next town would be Abilene, two to three months away.

Stone crawled into his bunk and pulled his scratchy wool blanket over his shoulders. Truscott was like an old sergeant major, and Stone one of the troopers, not the young captain who gave orders to the sergeant major.

Thursday morning he was going up the trail, and by the time he got to Abilene, he'd know everything necessary to go into the cattle business. He closed his eyes, and drifted off into the deep restful slumber that comes to the lucky man who's made love to a passionate woman that day. A chorus of wheezes and snores surrounded him in the darkened bunkhouse as the full moon threw spears through the windows and the *segundo* cuddled up to his dog.

Around midnight, Gideon Whiteside rode his bay onto the grounds of his ranch, and saw all the lights out in the windows. He urged the bay into the stable, dismounted, loosened the cinch, and put the horse in a stall. Tomorrow morning one of the cowboys could remove the saddle and blanket. Whiteside didn't feel like taking the time, because he was tired.

He walked toward the main house, wearing his dusty frock coat and wide curve-brimmed hat, the empty sleeve dangling weirdly in the breeze. He hadn't wanted to come back, but thought it necessary to allay any suspicions Cassandra might have. He'd leave soon as he had the count's money in his hand, and to hell with Cassandra and this pathetic excuse for a ranch.

He climbed the steps to the porch and opened the front door, stepping into the darkened living room. A ray of moonlight shone onto the painting of himself in the colonel's uniform, and somehow he'd like to take it with him when he left, because it impressed people and added resonance to his charade.

He climbed the stairs to the second floor, made his way through the shadows to the room he shared with Cassandra, and went inside.

The window was open, and the breeze fluttered the white curtains. Cassandra lay on her stomach, wearing a thin white cotton nightgown, and Whiteside undressed silently, because he didn't want to waken her.

"Is that you, Gideon?" she asked sleepily.

"Who else were you expecting, my dear?" he asked jovially, and then bent toward her, kissing her cheek.

"I'd like to speak with you, if you don't mind."

"Not now, dear. It's late."

"I'm afraid it can't wait."

She arose and lit the lamp, suffusing the room with a golden glow. Her face was pale, hair mussed, and eyes half-closed, but she still was beautiful, he could see that, though not as beautiful as Rosalie.

"Anything wrong?" he asked, peeling off his shirt, showing the gray hairs on his chest and the bulge of stomach.

"I'm afraid there is," Cassandra said. "Ten thousand dollars is missing from our accounts."

Gideon put a mystified expression on his face. "What happened?"

"You sent it to the Denver Investor's Syndicate—don't you remember?"

"Oh, that," he said with a munificent wave of his hand. "I remember now."

"What was the money for?"

"A solid investment that might very well make us rich someday."

"An investment in what?"

"Silver mines in Colorado. If just one of them hits the mother lode, we'll be able to buy Texas."

"Why didn't you tell me?"

He threw the shirt over the chair and stood bare-chested before her, the stump of his arm grotesque in the light of the lamp. "I didn't think it was important," he explained. "It was only ten thousand dollars, not a lot of money, and I wanted to surprise you, dear, when we struck the mother lode."

He moved toward her, wrapped his arm around her waist, and kissed her cheek, but she pushed him away gently, and he was surprised, because usually she was a fool for affection.

"This *is* a surprise, Gideon," she said, "and ten thousand dollars really is quite a lot of money. You've put us in rather a bad situation. Can't you get the money back?"

"You couldn't expect me to back out of a deal, could you? I mean, my reputation is on the line here."

Her heart was beating like a tom-tom, and she felt light-headed, as if she were going to faint. "I know about the house in San Antone," she said softly.

"What house is that?" he asked.

"The house you bought for Miss Rosalie Cowper, on Chestnut Street."

There was silence for a few seconds as they stared at each other across the bed. He wracked his mind for a response; he was an old flimflam man, had appeared in many plays, and could represent the full spectrum of a man's moods.

He sighed, went limp, and dropped into a chair. "I know what you're thinking," he said, "but it's not true. Miss Rosalie Cowper is the daughter of Captain Digby Cowper, my operations officer during the war. Captain Cowper fell at Sharpsburg, shielding my body from shrapnel with his own body. He lost his life, and I only lost my arm, but perhaps it would've been better the other way around, I don't know.

"A short time ago, through a series of odd circumstances, I happened to meet his daughter in town, and she was destitute. I felt it incumbent upon me, as an officer and a gentleman, to help her, so I bought her that house. No matter what happens to her now, at least she'll have a roof over her head, and that's the least I can do for the daughter of the man who saved my life. But, my dear, I thought we could afford it."

"If she was destitute, what did she do with the money she earns as a dancer in the Last Chance Saloon?"

Whiteside had no plausible answer, so the time had come to change the texture of his performance. He rose to his feet and banged the heel of his fist on the dresser.

"How dare you hurl these accusations at me, as if I were a common philanderer! What did you expect me to do when

I saw the poor suffering daughter of the man who'd saved my life? Should I've turned my back on her? Why how can you even, in your wildest dreams, think there'd be anything improper between that child and me? It hurts me deeply, Cassandra, to know that you have so little faith in me. Evidently it's not enough for a soldier to lose his arm on the field of battle. He has to be insulted and vilified as well, and be called a common thief by his own wife who swore, before God, not more than two years ago, to love and cherish him forever! Very well, if that's what you think of me, I might as well leave, and join the other poor homeless soldiers roaming the frontier, taking our chances on the roulette wheel of life! I never dreamed I'd see the day when my own darling Cassandra would become a jealous petty shrew!"

Is that what I've become? she asked herself. *Have I unjustly accused my husband?* It was a plausible enough story—he'd helped the child of an old comrade. Gideon never had been knowledgeable about business, and would have no concept of the havoc he'd wreaked.

While Whiteside had been talking, he searched for a better way to sell his story, like any flimflam man trapped in a corner. "You asked before," he said, "why she was out of funds while working as a dancer. The reason is she was sick much of last year, and couldn't work. Her situation was quite desperate when I ran into her, and although it's not polite to say, I must tell you that she was on the verge of becoming a prostitute. I've saved her from that, and if I was wrong, I'll submit willingly to the judgment of God, but as for the money, Cassandra, you know there are some things, like honor and decency, that are far more important than mere filthy lucre!"

She wanted to believe him, so she did, because the alternative was too horrible and ugly. "Please forgive me, Gideon," she said, "but I've been under tremendous strain lately."

She ran toward him, and he took her in his arm.

"I understand, my dear," he replied. "These are difficult times. People of honor have nowhere to turn."

"I realize you don't know anything about business," she said, laying her head on his hairy chest, "but we're in trouble because of that investment. I don't think you realize the gravity of the situation, but we've got to get our cattle out of here before the creditors take them away."

He patted her head with his hand, as though she were a cocker spaniel. "I'm sure you'll take care of everything, my dear. You're a bright girl. What do you propose?"

"I've already given orders to Truscott. We're leaving for Abilene day after tomorrow."

His hand froze in the air. "So soon?"

"We can't wait. If the creditors get to the herd before we leave, there won't be anything left, and they'll take the land and buildings too. We'll be penniless, homeless, at the mercy of the elements."

"Is the herd formed?"

"Not yet."

"When did you give Truscott the order?"

"Tonight."

"He can't possibly get the herd moving that quickly."

"We'll move whatever he's got."

His features sagged, and his eyes became calculating. If she moved the herd in two days, he wouldn't be able to sell it to the count. He returned to the chair and put on his shirt.

"Where are you going?" she asked.

"Stay here," he replied, and it was more a command than a request.

He put on his hat and left the bedroom, slamming the door behind him, his lips quivering with rage. How dare she give orders to Truscott without consulting with him first? The woman didn't know her place in the marriage, but he'd show her, by God, after he finished in the bunkhouse.

He crossed the yard, swinging his arm back and forth, his lips pinched in determination. He'd lose Rosalie if the herd left before the count could buy it.

He threw open the door of the bunkhouse and marched inside. "Truscott!" he boomed.

There were grunts and moans underneath the blankets, but no one said anything. Drawing his Colt, he pointed it at the ceiling, drew back the hammer with his thumb, and pulled the trigger.

The shot echoed throughout the bunkhouse, and everybody went for his gun.

"This is Colonel Whiteside speaking! Somebody get Truscott! It's an emergency!"

Whiteside holstered his gun as the bunkhouse came to life. He lit a match with his thumbnail and gave light to the lamp in the middle of the table, amid the deck of cards, dirty dishes, and assorted cruddy eating utensils. Thorpe ran out the door to get Truscott.

Whiteside turned and saw his cowboys gathered around him, carrying guns, quizzical expressions on their faces. Whiteside held himself erectly and stared them down. A few moments later Truscott entered the bunkhouse, his hair and mustache awry, a Colt in his hand.

Whiteside placed his hand on his hip and stood with one foot in front of him, like a ghastly old thespian giving the performance of his life.

"Ramrod," he said in his deepest baritone voice, "my wife gave you an order this evening that was a mistake. The herd is *not* going up the trail on the day after tomorrow, or any other day in the foreseeable future. Furthermore, hereafter you'll take all your orders from me, and if my wife tells you anything, ignore her. There are some things she simply doesn't understand. Do I make myself clear?"

Outside, standing at the window, Cassandra's jaw was hanging open in shock. She'd followed him across the yard, heard every word he'd said, and couldn't believe her ears. It was the worst nightmare of her life coming true, the man she loved not simply betraying her but also trying to ruin her.

She'd believed him, forgiven him, apologized for her accusations, and now the horror had returned with additional momentum. Her head spun with pain, and she wanted to fall down and cry, but something deep inside her said don't give up without a fight.

All she knew was she had to stop him. She didn't have a strategy prepared, a speech tucked into her pocket, or any concept whatever of what to do, but penultimate in her mind was the fear that if she didn't stop him, she might end up as a prostitute in the Last Chance Saloon.

She reached for the doorknob as Truscott told Whiteside: "You're the boss. The herd stays where it is." He turned and faced the men. "We're not goin' up the trail, so forget about goin' to town for supplies, and I'll tell you yer jobs in the mornin'."

The door was flung open, and Cassandra entered the bunk-house. She wore a white robe over her nightdress, and the belt was tied tightly, revealing the outline of her slim waist, while her bosom surged against the cotton and silk.

Whiteside spun around and stared at her. *"I told you to stay in your room!"*

She didn't even look at him as she advanced in her slippers toward Truscott, and the eyes of every cowboy followed her across a floor strewn with cigarette butts, chicken bones, scraps of paper, and thick whorls of dust.

"Mr. Truscott," she said, "this is my ranch, not my husband's. I paid for it with my own money, and I can prove it. I gave you an order this evening, and I expect you to carry it out *as we discussed.*"

Truscott looked back and forth between them, scratched his head, and said, "Mebbe both of you should see a lawyer and get this thing straightened out, because I don't know what to do."

"Well said!" Whiteside replied, puffing out his chest. "Let the courts decide!" He knew it would take months and maybe even years before the courts would settle the matter, and by then he'd be long gone with Rosalie and the money.

Cassandra knew the same thing, and she had to get the herd moving. "There isn't time for the courts. We'll settle everything after I sell the herd in Abilene, but if we don't get the herd moving, there won't be anything to settle."

She saw that Truscott was baffled, and the only thing to do was appeal to the men themselves. She turned and faced them, trying to fight back the tears, but one silvery orb rolled down her alabaster cheek.

"My husband is trying to ruin me," she said in a quavering voice. "I don't know why, but I believe it has something to do with a woman he's keeping in town. I'll be wiped out if he gets away with it, and I'm asking you to please do the right thing and help me."

Before she got the last word out of her mouth, she felt herself being flung across the room. She tripped, lost her footing, spun around, and crashed into the wall.

Gideon Whiteside stood before her, his shadow elongated by the light of the lantern.

"I told you," he said in a threatening voice, "to go back to your room!"

She picked herself up off the floor. "This is my home!" she replied. "And if you don't like what goes on here, then *you* leave!"

"Why you goddamn . . ."

He charged toward her, grabbed her hair, and whipped her around, sending her flying toward the door. Her back crashed against it, and he rushed at her, raising his fist, because he couldn't let a woman talk to him that way.

He brought his hand forward, to smack her as she'd never been smacked before, when a grip like iron caught his wrist and flung him aside.

Now he was the one struggling for balance, but he couldn't quite make it, dropping onto his rear end, but as soon as he landed, he jumped to his feet.

He spun around and saw John Stone, barefoot, wearing jeans and guns.

"Well," Whiteside said indignantly, "I guess you must feel proud of yourself, pushing around a man nearly twice your age, who gave his arm in the war!"

"Get on your horse," Stone replied, "and don't stop riding until you're off this range."

"Now just a minute," Whiteside replied. "You can't . . ."

"I'm not going to tell you again," Stone interrupted. "Get going, while you can walk."

Whiteside looked around, and saw the array of cowboys before him. For a moment he didn't understand, but then it came to him. They'd seen him strike a woman, and the fools naturally took her side. He realized he shouldn't have beaten her in front of them, because ignorant people misunderstand things.

But Whiteside always believed he had tremendous acting ability. Hadn't he fooled the world with his war hero act? Perhaps, like Marc Antony, he could turn the fickle crowd around.

"Gentlemen," he said, striking a noble pose, "You've all been around long enough to know what women are like. They lie, they cheat, and all they want to do is put their hands into a man's pockets. That's what this one is doing to me, and I'm afraid it's got me a little worked up. Now I know what you're thinking right now, that she's sweet and nice, and it can't be true, but underneath those blond curls and angelic features lives a little devil trying to steal everything I own, so she can give it to"—he pointed to John Stone—"this man here, who wears a Confederate cavalry officer's hat, but unless I miss my guess was a deserter!"

Everybody looked at Stone, and Whiteside was surprised to see the maze of crisscrossed scratches on Stone's back.

"This man is a crook!" Stone said. "We ought to run him out of here!"

Truscott raised his hand. "Now just a minute! Don't get yer balls in an uproar! If this ranch belongs to this man, and we run him off, we'll have the Texas Rangers on our asses, and I, for one, am not lookin' to take on the Texas Rangers!"

The cowboys argued among themselves, as Cassandra climbed to her feet. A trickle of blood showed at the corner of her mouth, and her robe and gown were torn, revealing half her left breast, but the worst pain was deep in her heart, and it kept getting worse.

She had to save the herd, but didn't know what to say to the men. They were accustomed to taking orders from Truscott, and now she regretted being aloof from them, because she hardly knew any of them personally, and for all they knew she was just another bitch trying to steal a man's money.

Then one of the men, the tall string bean who played the guitar, raised his hand. "I got somethin' to say!"

Everybody looked at him, because he so seldom said anything. Mostly he strummed his guitar, lost in old tunes of trails and cows and men who ended up in Boot Hill.

He stepped forward nervously, in long dirty white underwear, and he too had strapped on his iron and wore his battered hat.

"I was in town today," he said. "I know I wasn't supposed to go, and I should've been lookin' for strays on the range north of here, but I went anyways, because I needed me a drink of whiskey, and I thought I'd have me a woman, because I . . ."

Truscott interrupted him. "What's yer goddamned point, you asshole!"

"I passed out on a bench near City Hall, and was woke up by some drunk cowboys from the Diamond D talkin' about us, the crew here at the Triangle Spur, sayin' we was no good, and dumb, and we don't know nothin' 'bout cattle, but Mrs. Whiteside was there, and she stuck up for us. Now understand me, these cowboys were armed, but she didn't care, and she told 'em *'we was as fine a bunch of cowboys as ever rode the range'*!" He paused. "That's what she said, and I thought you all might want to know, because for my part, I agree with John Stone here, and I say we ought to run this bigmouthed son of a bitch out of here! Any man who hits a woman, in my opinion, is a goddamned coward!"

There was silence for a few moments. The cowboys looked at Whiteside, then at Cassandra, then back to Whiteside. Stone decided the tide had turned in Cassandra's favor, and he had to act before the men changed their minds.

He drew his guns and aimed them at Whiteside. "Get going."

"Young man," Whiteside replied, "you keep on that way, and you'll end up with a rope around your neck."

Stone pulled the trigger of one of his Colts, and the floorboards exploded at Whiteside's feet, making him jump backward.

"I said get moving."

"Now see here!"

Stone pulled both triggers, and splinters flew into the air around the old ham, who assumed his formal actor's posture once more, although his hand was trembling. "You're going to pay for that!" he hollered.

Stone walked toward him, aiming both guns at Whiteside's head, and the bunkhouse crowd followed him, guns in their hands. Whiteside realized he hadn't swayed them, and maybe he wasn't such a great actor after all. Stone came to a halt in front of him, and pointed his guns at his eyes.

"You're the scum of the earth," Stone said to him. "Get off this property, and if you come back with the Rangers, I'm sure Mrs. Whiteside will have a lot to tell them."

A bright flash of hatred passed between them, and Whiteside could see he was outgunned and outmanned. There was nothing to do but leave with his head held high, like the great hero he believed he was, because Whiteside wasn't sure what was real anymore, and sometimes thought he really had commanded a battalion in the old Stonewall Brigade.

Like a proud warrior, he turned and marched toward the door, glaring hatefully at Cassandra as he passed.

It was silent in the bunkhouse as they listened to his footsteps receding into the distance, then Stone looked at Cassandra, his eyes roving over her pulped lips, which looked like rosebuds in the light of the lantern.

She stepped toward the men standing in a phalanx before her, half-dressed, guns in their hands. "I want to thank you for your help," she said, tears in her eyes. "I know I haven't been very nice in the past, but I was afraid of you, yet I watched and admired you from a distance, and hoped you'd like me. When I was in town today, and said you were fine men, I suppose I didn't know what I was talking about, but now that I've seen you close up, I can say with all my heart that you truly are the finest men to ever ride the range, and the finest men I've ever met in my life!"

There wasn't a dry eye in the bunkhouse, and even the *segundo*'s low cur was melancholy, his ears lying back on his head, a sad whine emitting from his strangled vocal chords.

Truscott extended his arm. "I'll walk you back to yer house, ma'am, and I think I'd better leave a few of the men there with you, in case that son of a bitch husband of yours decides to come back." He turned toward the men. "I want three volunteers."

Every man raised his hand and stepped forward, and Cassandra couldn't suppress a smile.

"First time anyone ever volunteered for anythin' around here," said Truscott. "Guess I'll have to pick three. Unless you want to, ma'am."

"I'd trust your judgment, Mr. Truscott."

"Thorpe, Slipchuck, John Stone. Take Mrs. Whiteside home, and if you see that one-armed son of a bitch . . ."

Slipchuck waved his six-gun. "We'll take care of him, Ramrod."

The three cowboys dressed while the others drifted back toward their bunks. Cassandra looked at a chair, and it was covered with stains of questionable provenance, but she was tired, and sat upon it.

She still was dazed, not by the power of Gideon's punches, but by the fact that he'd struck her at all. The gleam in his eyes had been vicious, and if the cowboys hadn't been there, he probably would've beaten her quite badly.

No longer could she have delusions about Whiteside. The man obviously was pure malevolent evil, lying to her from the first day. And she'd swallowed it hook, line, and sinker. *How could I've been so stupid?*

Now, for the first time, she could see what a pompous fool he was, but there was a touch of the demonic in him too, and maybe it was more than just a touch.

There was no time to worry about mistakes of the past. They had to move the herd out.

Meanwhile, toward the back of the bunkhouse, Stone reached into his saddlebags and pulled out a clean shirt, but something fell out along with it.

It was the picture of Marie, and he held it in the light. He hadn't thought about her for a while, but now here she was again. A peculiar chill went through him as he looked from the picture to Cassandra Whiteside sitting in the squalor of the bunkhouse. He stuffed the picture deep into the cavernous saddlebag, put on his hat, and walked toward the front of the bunkhouse, passing the men in their bunks staring respectfully, and maybe a little lustfully, at Cassandra Whiteside.

Stone came to a stop in front of her, and she looked up at him. "I can't believe what he's done to me," she said, a lost note in her voice.

"The man's full of bullshit, Cassandra. What did you expect?"

"He didn't seem full of bullshit to me. Why was I so blind?"

"You didn't know any better, but now you do, and you'll never do it again."

It gave her comfort to know he was right, she'd never trust another man like Whiteside, but it was too early to think of other men, because first, and most importantly, she had to get that herd moving.

She turned to John Stone and looked at his profile as he peered out the window. His hat was low over his eyes, and his muscles strained at his clothing. She recalled that he was the first one to speak out for her, when she and Whiteside had been fighting for the allegiance of the men, and that had been the major turning point in the struggle.

She recalled the night she and Gideon had supper with Stone, and she'd thought Stone had been a charming nonentity compared to Gideon, but now, with her new perspective, she realized that Gideon had been a buffoon, while Stone was a true gentleman, and evidently saw through her husband like a pane of glass.

She gazed at Stone with renewed interest, as Slipchuck and Thorpe moved toward the front of the bunkhouse. Rising from her chair, she faced the cowboys and said, "Good night, men, and thank you again for your help."

She blew out the lantern and walked toward the door, followed by Slipchuck, Thorpe, and John Stone.

The horses were restless in the corral, snorting and shaking their heads as they watched the woman and three men walk from the bunkhouse to the main house.

They'd heard the shots and sounds of fighting, and hadn't known what to expect. Every horse in the corral had suffered due to the antics of cowboys. Some had been caught in fires set by drunken cowboys, and barely escaped with their lives. Others had been in the middle of pitched gunfights. A few had belonged to outlaws and spent literally years running from the law. Nearly half had been stolen at least once in their lives, and many had received cruel treatment from owners.

Every horse in the corral had been awakened from a deep sleep in the middle of the night and forced to run somewhere at top speed. Tonight?

The woman and three men entered the main house, and lanterns went on. It was silent, and the horses hoped the rest of the night would be peaceful, but everything could change suddenly, you could never tell.

The lights went out, and the only illumination came from the moon and stars. Tomahawk stood near the rail, looking at the house, aware that John Stone was there.

Tomahawk had spent all day in the corral, and hoped to get out tomorrow. But now the ranch was still. The people had gone to sleep.

He turned away, and saw the palomino mare ten feet away, looking at him. He moved toward her, admiring her smooth coat and the sheen of her flanks. They'd been maneuvering around each other all day, and now all the cowboys were asleep.

Tomahawk gazed at the palomino, and when their eyes met, it was like staring at the sun. Tomahawk flicked his tail and moved toward her.

8

GIDEON WHITESIDE SPENT the night alone on the prairie, near a stream that sang merrily as he tossed and turned on his bedroll, trying to fall asleep.

The ground was hard, unlike the soft feather bed he'd slept in with Cassandra, and his saddle was no substitute for the plump pillow he'd enjoyed. If it rained, he'd be miserable, but it wouldn't be the first time. He'd spent many nights sleeping under train trestles, or in alleyways or open fields. He was no stranger to hardship, but his two years with Cassandra had softened him.

He became furious when he thought of Cassandra. She had humiliated him, and the men had sided with her, because all they saw was her pretty face.

Men couldn't think straight around women, who were witches, clouding men's minds, making them insane. The cowboys would do anything she said, especially when she started crying. What could a man do when a woman cried?

Whiteside would've walloped her again, if he'd had the chance. She needed it if any woman ever did. How dare she defy him? She'd pay for it, and there was only one sum he'd take: her life.

He was going to kill her, first chance he got. He'd find her alone somewhere and cut her throat. But not too quickly. He'd do it slowly, so she could feel every tear of the knife, so she'd

149

know she'd challenged the wrong man.

He balled his fists underneath the blanket and grit his teeth. If there's anything a flimflam man hates, it's when his mask is torn away, and he stands naked before the crowd.

If I have to follow her to the end of the earth, I'll do it. She'll never escape me.

Cassandra sat by her open window, gazing out at the wide prairie stretched endlessly beneath the shower of stars.

Her lips were tender, and a few teeth were loose in her mouth. She had black and blue marks, but otherwise no serious damage except for the deep depression that had overtaken her as soon as she'd returned to her room.

She felt like a moron for believing in Gideon so completely and reverently. She realized she knew nothing about him except what he'd told her, and she'd always believed him because she'd never dreamed that a man who'd lost his arm in the war could be a villain.

Now she realized he might not've been in the war at all. His arm could've been lost by any number of accidents, and it wasn't his arm that was the problem anyway. It was his soul, or his lack of one. And he'd fooled her completely.

She had to admit he'd fooled other people too. He'd been highly regarded in New Orleans, although now that she thought of it, many of the better citizens had nothing to do with him. She'd thought it simple snobbery at the time, but now realized they'd seen through him, as John Stone did.

John Stone. The big cowboy strode into her mind, with his easy gait and wide rolling shoulders. She'd thought him the wreckage of a young man, but he was the first to step forward for her. Maybe he could drive her wagon all the way to Abilene, and they could get to know each other better.

She realized she was being an idiot again. Every available cowboy would be needed for the drive. She'd have to drive her own wagon to Abilene, and she'd learn on the trail.

What would she take with her? She realized she'd been gazing out the window at the moon when she should be preparing for the drive. She had to pack, check supplies, close down the house, a million things to do. *Why am I sitting here?*

She lit the lamp, and the first decision to make was what to wear. It was going to be an ordeal, so she'd need her most durable clothing. Those were her riding outfits, which essentially were cowboy outfits tailored to her womanly proportions. She opened a drawer and took out a pair of jeans, while in another drawer she found a cotton shirt covered with small red and white checks.

She dressed in the light of the lamp, then sat on the chair and pulled on her cowboy boots. Standing in front of the mirror, she appraised herself. Would the men take orders from this person? She put on her cowboy hat and adjusted the neck strap. Maybe they'd laugh at her. It wasn't going to be easy, but somehow they had to get the herd to Abilene.

Dawn broke over the Diamond D Ranch as Gideon Whiteside rode toward the count's residence. He hadn't slept much, had eaten no breakfast, and the only thing keeping him going was his hatred for Cassandra.

He'd washed in a stream and brushed the dust off his clothing, but was unshaven, his hair uncombed, and looked grubby as his horse stopped in front of the rail.

Whiteside climbed down, threw the reins over the rail, climbed onto the front porch, knocked on the door, and it was opened by a liveried butler.

"I'd like to see the count. Tell him it's extremely important."

"This way, sir."

Whiteside sat on a chair, crossed his legs, and lit a thin cigar. He'd spent most of the night planning what he'd say to the count, because without the count's money, Whiteside's prospects were dim indeed.

He knew the count didn't like him, and probably even held him in contempt, therefore he had to convince the count that it was in *his* best interest to buy the Triangle Spur for a mere fraction of its worth, but enough to remove Rosalie and himself to St. Louis in style.

And when he was established in St. Louis, he'd find another woman to pay his bills, while he maintained Rosalie in a discreet home someplace. He could visit her a few times a week, for communal bathing.

"The count will see you now, sir."

Whiteside followed the butler up the stairs and down a corridor to a large plush room with a bed covered by a canopy. Count Von Falkenheim sat near the window, his head leaned back on a pillow, as another gentleman shaved him.

Whiteside walked toward him and bowed slightly. "I apologize for disturbing you at this ungodly hour, Your Excellency, but a matter of great importance has come up, which I thought would be of interest to you, and I . . ."

"Out with it," said the count, his jowls covered with lather. "I do not haf much time."

"Of course you don't. I realize full well how busy you are. I am here for one purpose only. I want to sell you not only my herd, but the entire Triangle Spur Ranch, with buildings, horses, equipment, saddles, wagons, everything there, for the incredible bargain price of only ten thousand dollars, but you must act fast, because my wife plans to move the herd to Kansas on the day after tomorrow."

"As I told you before, I do not understand American legalities. I vill haf to consult vith a lawyer."

"A deal like this comes along once in a lifetime, and besides, I can tell you the law. In this country, a man can dispose of his property however he wants."

"Even if the property belongs to his vife?"

"Correct."

"That is the vay it is in my country too."

"It's the only way, but my wife is trying to defy me."

The count gazed at him with naked scorn. "Somebody ought to defy you, because you are an utter svine."

"You don't have to like me," Whiteside said. "Just remember that the Triangle Spur is worth far more than the price I quoted, and you know it. You could greatly increase your range and expand your operations. You're here to turn a profit, aren't you, or are you just passing time?"

The barber finished the shave and washed the lather away as the count reflected upon what Whiteside had said. It was true that he was there to turn a profit. His family's money was invested in the ranch, and it was his duty to increase the value of the investment. It certainly was an attractive offer, if it was legal.

"Vhy are you doing this to your vife, Vhiteside? I always thought she vas rather sveet, although I must confess I never knew vhat she saw in you."

"She's a sneaky little traitor."

The count accepted the towel from his servant, and dried his face. "You cannot control your vife?"

"The cowboys sided with her. They think she's sweet, as you do."

"You are a clever talker, Vhiteside. I vould think you could vin them over, if she is as dumb as you say."

"I was doing all right, until John Stone stepped in."

"Who?"

"One of the cowboys. He's probably in love with her, like all the rest of the idiots."

"I do not believe I know him. Is he one of your new hands?"

"A former officer who's deteriorated since the war, but evidently he's influential with the men, damn him. He looked like he'd been in a fight with a wildcat. His back was scratched to shreds."

The count stiffened in his chair. "Vhat did you say?"

"His back was covered with scratches. It really looked quite bad. Never seen anything quite like it. Must've been one of local whores, and I wish I knew her name."

The count arose from his chair, unbuttoned his shirt, and turned around. "Did it look like this?"

Whiteside stared in shock at the count's back, because it looked just like John Stone's. "Yes."

The count put his shirt back on. "Where is this John Stone?"

The herd stretched like a vast living carpet on the measureless prairie as the cowboys approached on horseback. It was a sunny day with a few puffy clouds in the sky, and a flock of birds darted overhead, chasing a swarm of insects.

Stone rode between Blakemore and Duvall, toward the back of the crew.

"Wish we had a few more days," Duvall said, "so's I could git married."

"What the hell you want to git married for?" Blakemore asked, his Yankee forage cap tilted rakishly on the side of his head. "It's askin' to be locked in jail."

"I wouldn't mind bein' locked someplace with Eulalie," Duvall said. "My idea of heaven."

"That's what you're sayin' now, but after you're married awhile, and she gits to naggin', you'll be on yer way back to that cave."

Stone puffed a cigarette and examined the cattle, which chomped grass and looked at him curiously as he passed, sitting tall in his saddle. He felt terrific, on the open range at last, learning the cattle business, and one day he'd have a herd of his own, a home with a wife and kids, dogs and cats, and chickens in the backyard. It wasn't much to hope for. A lot of men did it. And he'd do it too, once he learned cattle.

Truscott raised his hand, and the cowboys pulled their horses to a stop behind him. The ramrod wheeled his horse so he could face them, and said, "You see all them cattle down there?" He pointed with his gloved hand. "Well, some of 'em's ours and some ain't. We got to cut ours out, bring 'em back here, and then take 'em to the main herd. We ain't got much time, so's we might as well git started. Make sure you don't cut any that ain't ours. Any questions?"

The cowboys drifted into the valley, and Stone was surprised by the lack of instructions he'd received. He didn't know exactly what to do, and figured he'd just copy the others.

He rode among the scattered cattle, and saw a variety of brands, with many mavericks among them. If he had a branding iron, he could put it on all the mavericks he found, and they'd be his herd.

The cattle gazed dully at him as he passed. He spotted the brand of the Triangle Spur on the left side of a steer, and touched his spurs to Tomahawk's flanks. "Let's go, boy."

Tomahawk didn't need prodding. He'd been cutting cattle most of his life, and had seen the Triangle Spur brand first. He bounded toward it, and the steer tried to get out of his way. Tomahawk shifted direction, and the steer realized the only thing to do was run, so he turned and moved in the direction Tomahawk wanted him to go. The cowboys yipped and yelled, waving their hats in the air, and Stone joined the chorus of human and animal sounds, a real cowboy at last.

Ten gunfighters were seated on sofas and chairs in Von Falkenheim's living room, as a butler served them tea and cakes.

The gunfighters were dressed like cowboys, but somehow didn't look like cowboys. They were hard men with cruel eyes, and they earned their living not by herding cows, but by killing men.

They dreamed not of their own ranch, but of how to shave a split second off the time it'd take to draw and fire. They didn't want a wife and family, but a high price for their fast hands. They preferred to be paid for a skill they only used occasionally, but whenever they used it, Boot Hill was never far away.

They'd rather gamble with death than work for a living, and the most deadly among them was Dave Quarternight, who had slanted eyes, high cheekbones, and a long sallow face. He was six feet tall, and looked like a snake coiled on a chair.

They heard footsteps in the corridor, and moments later Von Falkenheim marched into the living room, wearing black polished Prussian riding boots. He looked at his gunfighters, placed his fists on his hips, and said, "The time has come for you to earn your pay. This morning I haf bought the Triangle Spur, undt ve're going over now to move the herd closer to this range. There might be trupple, so stay close to me, and follow my orders carefully."

Quarternight grinned. "I don't think that bunch has much fight."

"Neither do I, but ve must be prepared. Everybody on your horse, except Quarternight." He looked meaningfully at Quarternight. "I vant to haf a few vords with you in private."

Quarternight nodded, and the gunfighters filed out of the living room, shuffling their boots, hitching their gunbelts. The door closed after the last one, and Von Falkenheim moved toward Quarternight, sitting in a chair opposite him.

"There is someone I vant you to kill," he said. "He is one of the Triangle Spur cowboys, undt his name is John Stone. Ever hear of him?"

Quarternight shook his head.

"I vill point him out to you. He is a big tall fellow, like you. Make him fight you. You know how to do it."

Quarternight nodded.

"Time to get started."

Von Falkenheim arose, put on his new pearl-gray cowboy hat, and made his way toward the door. He wore riding breeches, a black leather coat, and a gunbelt with a Colt in the holster. The butler opened the door, and Von Falkenheim stepped outside, followed by Quarternight.

Arrayed before him were twenty-six mounted cowboys and his crew of gunfighters, plus Gideon Whiteside. Von Falkenheim climbed onto his white Arabian stallion, and Quarternight swung himself over the saddle of his dun. Von Falkenheim galloped out of the yard, with Quarternight at his side, and the men fell in behind him, heading toward San Jacinto Valley.

Tomahawk worked a steer toward the gathering area, and the steer didn't want to go, but Tomahawk charged him again and again, cutting off his avenues of escape, and finally the steer gave up and trotted sullenly toward the others being held by the *segundo*.

Stone sat in his saddle, taking deep draughts of prairie atmosphere. Now he could understand why men loved to be cowboys. It was a healthy life in the great outdoors, and was great fun if you loved riding horses.

Stone had been riding practically from the time he could walk, and that's why he'd joined the cavalry. Now he could see his destiny before him more clearly than ever. He'd be a cowboy until he knew enough to form his own herd, and then the sky'd be the limit.

Tomahawk turned back toward the herd, and Stone realized he didn't feel a need for a drink or dancing girls. He was perfectly happy working cattle, and could feel his appetite building. The great thing about being a cowboy was you'd never go hungry, with all those prime tenderloin steaks walking around.

He had the feeling he finally knew what to do with the rest of his life, as the steer plodded toward the holding area, and the bright sun blazed across the clear blue sky.

Cassandra and Agnes were carrying boxes down the stairs when Agnes perked up her ears. "Somebody's comin'!" she said.

They placed the boxes on the floor, ran for the rifles, and took positions at the windows. They could be Indians, outlaws, or the first creditors arriving to take the herd away!

They gazed out over the prairie and saw a buckboard approaching through clouds of dust.

"It's the cook!" Agnes shouted.

They relaxed their fingers on the triggers and leaned the rifles against the wall, returning to the boxes. Cassandra was only taking a few articles of clothing, some books, and kitchen utensils. She'd have to travel light and move quickly, not be a burden to the men.

She knew the men didn't want her to go with them, because she'd make them feel inhibited, but she'd stay away and let them do anything that was all right with Truscott. She knew men didn't like to take orders from women, and had no desire to rile them. The main thing was to get the herd moving before the creditors came.

They placed the last box near the door, and Agnes wiped her brow with the back of her hand. "That's about it for what's upstairs," she said.

"All that's left is the office," Cassandra replied. "You prepare lunch, while I decide what to take."

There was a knock on the door. Agnes opened it, and Thorpe stood there, covered with the dust of the trail.

"The cook's goin' on out to San Jacinto Valley," he said, "and we decided I should stay here with you all, to look out fer you."

Cassandra looked at him, and he was little more than a boy. "No, that's all right," she said. "We need everyone with the herd. Agnes and I can take care of ourselves."

"Don't think that's a good idea, if you don't mind me sayin' so," Thorpe said. "No tellin' what might happen."

"Nothing will happen. Please report to Mr. Truscott."

Thorpe walked away, and Agnes closed the door. Cassandra made her way down the hallway to her office, wondering what was necessary for the trip.

The deed to the ranch was the most important document, and bank records were next. Then she found her marriage certificate, and held it up to the light, examining her signature and that of Gideon Whiteside along with the preacher who'd married them.

She'd thought Gideon was a great man—why? Because he'd looked like a great man, and sounded like one? How could a person know the truth about another person just by looking and listening? Somehow John Stone had done it. She'd have to ask him about it sometime.

She gathered important papers, folding them into a brown leather briefcase, and then Agnes brought her lunch: a fried steak with potatoes and gravy. There was a knock on the door as she was finishing her second cup of tea.

"Come in!"

The door opened, and Ephraim stood there, the top three buttons of his shirt undone, his hat in hand. "I was about to leave with the chuck wagon, ma'am, and I was wonderin' if you needed anythin'."

"We're fine, Ephraim. I think you ought to go immediately. The more men with the herd, the better."

"Sure Thorpe can't stay wif you?"

"Agnes and I can take care of ourselves."

Ephraim cocked his head to one side, then reached into his pocket and took out a small ivory-handled derringer on a gold chain. "Maybe you'd better put this around yer neck," he said, "just in case."

She held the derringer in the palm of her hand and looked at it. "It's beautiful," she said. "Where did you get it?"

"An old man give it to me a long time ago."

"It looks expensive. I can't take something valuable like this."

"Give it back when we reach Abilene."

She dropped the gold chain around her neck, letting the derringer fall out of sight between her breasts. "You can be sure I'll take good care of it."

"Yes, ma'am, and it'll give you good luck too, because it was blessed by a priest who had powers, and could do miracles."

"What kind of miracles?"

"One time I seen him bring a dead body back to life."

Cassandra smiled, thinking Ephraim a well-intentioned but essentially ignorant and deluded child. "Tell Truscott that Agnes and I'll join the herd first thing in the morning, and we'll have breakfast with you. I'm looking forward to your cooking, Ephraim."

"Mebbe you should fire a few practice shots with the derringer, to make sure you knows how to use it," Ephraim suggested.

He left the office, and Cassandra returned to her cup of tea. There was something interesting about Ephraim, and he had a body a sculptor would love, but no, it was impossible, Cassandra refused even to think about it.

She returned to the papers on her desk, culling through them, trying to figure what was important and what could be left behind for the Comanches, who'd undoubtedly loot and burn the house down while she was gone.

Count Wolfgang Von Falkenheim, atop his white Arabian stallion, led his men toward San Jacinto Valley. The day was sunny and warm, and a buzzard circled in the sky above them, wondering if there'd be dead meat at the end of their ride. There were nearly forty of them, armed to the teeth, and they knew dirty work was ahead, but dirty work was a man's job, you couldn't escape it.

The ten gunfighters rode in a single rank behind Count Von Falkenheim, and were confident they could handle anything that lay ahead. Cowboys tended to avoid fights when the odds were against them, and that's what they expected in San Jacinto Valley.

Dave Quarternight rode near Von Falkenheim, a thin cheroot between his teeth, thinking about the man he'd kill. He didn't know him, but it was best that way. Knowing could set him thinking, and a gunfighter wanted to draw with nothing in the way.

Quarternight wondered who the poor fool would be. Probably another bowlegged cowboy with cowshit under his fingernails, who wouldn't have a chance. It gave Quarternight a charge whenever he killed somebody, so he looked forward to the encounter. Everybody treated him more respectfully, buying him drinks, patting his back, and sometimes a stray whore would screw him for the experience.

It amused him to know everybody was afraid of him, even Von Falkenheim, with all his money. Quarternight couldn't read or write, and his family didn't come from royalty, but he could shoot, and that was more important.

Before him rode Von Falkenheim, sitting erectly on his Arabian stallion, thinking about Veronika, how she'd betrayed him and how she'd pay. He felt she'd dishonored him and his proud name, by sleeping with a common cowboy. Stone would be killed that very day, but Veronika's fate would be far more cruel. He hadn't figured out exactly what it would be, but maybe he'd have his cowboys kidnap and rape her to death on the prairie, while he watched, a bottle of cognac in his hand. The more he held that image in his mind, the better he liked it. Not a bad idea, he thought.

At the rear of the cowboys, riding in the dust kicked up by their horses' hooves, his white silk handkerchief tied over his nose, sat Gideon Whiteside astride his bay.

He was thinking about Cassandra, how she'd embarrassed him, and it rankled. He was amazed at how quickly he'd sunk down in the world. Two days ago he was a respected rancher, and today he was eating the dust of the count's cowboys. Whiteside felt like a toad, and it was all Cassandra's fault.

But she'd pay. The count would take her cattle, and she'd probably become a prostitute, although she had all the passion of a bowl of oatmeal. And one night, when she least expected it, he'd bop her on the head, tie her to a bedpost, and slit her throat slowly, so she'd feel every tug of the knife.

Then she'd know she'd made the biggest mistake of her life, when she dared stand up to the hero of Sharpsburg. Whiteside thought of Cassandra's blood staining the sheets of her bed as he followed the count's men toward San Jacinto Valley.

The cowboys cut two hundred head of Triangle Spur cattle out of the mixed herd, and at midday drove them toward the main herd in San Jacinto Valley.

The small herd was stretched out in a long sinuous line, with Truscott in front on the point, and his more experienced cowboys riding on the sides as swing men or flankers.

Stone, Blakemore, and Duvall rode the drag, which was the position at the rear of the herd where dust was thickest. Coughing and spitting, they chased stragglers and tried to keep the slower cattle moving along steadily.

Stone saw that the more status a cowboy had, the farther forward he rode on the drive. That's why Truscott was in front, like a colonel commanding a regiment, and Stone was in the back, a raw recruit. But it wasn't unbearable, and no one shot at him. He had to work his way up from the bottom, and maybe someday he'd become a top hand, riding in front where the air was cleanest, steering the herd to Kansas.

In the late afternoon they came to San Jacinto Valley, and merged their small herd with the large one already gathered. It was the first time Stone had seen the main herd, and it stretched nearly to the horizon. The cattle were outlandish creatures with wide horns, drooling from black mouths, flicking their tails in the air.

Duvall was picked to be a guard, and Stone and Blakemore rode with the others toward the chuck wagon on the northern edge of the herd,. The chuck wagon would ride on the point near Truscott, so the dust wouldn't get into food and utensils.

"What do you think of your first day as a cowboy?" Blakemore asked, his nose and mouth covered with his bandanna, and his Yankee forage cap caked with dust.

"Not so bad," Stone replied, "but I wouldn't want to ride the drag for the rest of my life."

"You notice them mavericks back there? A man with a brandin' iron could have a herd in no time at all. Maybe you and me, and Duvall, ought to think about doin' somethin' like that when we git back from Abilene."

"I was thinking the same thing. The three of us together would be hard to beat."

"It looks like them greasers," Blakemore said, gazing toward the chuck wagon.

Stone turned his eyes in that direction and was surprised to see Don Emilio Maldonado and his vaqueros sitting near the fire. The closer Stone came, the worse they looked. Some were bloody and bandaged, and all looked as if they'd been riding hard. They rose to their feet, and Don Emilio limped slightly as he led his men toward Truscott and the cowboys from the Triangle Spur. A bloody swathe of white cotton fabric was wrapped around Don Emilio's forehead, causing his big sombrero to sit high on his head.

Truscott pulled back the reins of his horse and looked down at Don Emilio. "What the hell do you want?"

"Well, señor," Don Emilio explained, "it is like this. I owned a herd of my own in the brush country, but yesterday the Rangers came and said it was not mine. Then somebody started shooting, and my men and I were forced to leave *rapido* with only the clothes on our backs. Somebody told us you were looking for cowboys, so here we are, ready to work. We are all experienced vaqueros, and we will get your cattle to Abilene, do not worry about it."

Truscott knew about vaqueros from the brush country, and they were the toughest cowboys in the world. This bunch looked a little shot-up, and some were limping, but beggars couldn't be choosers.

"We can always use a few more good men," Truscott said, "but we can't pay you till we reach Abilene. You'll git yer chuck, though, and it'll be damn good."

"Excellente," Don Emilio said, and then he spotted Stone. "Look who is here!" he said. "The crazy gringo who knows how to use a knife!"

He walked toward Stone and held out his hand, but something else had caught Stone's eye. He was looking east, toward a huge cloud of dust approaching in the distance.

Everybody turned in that direction, and saw the cloud come closer. Stone pulled his old army spyglass out of his saddle-bags, raising it to his eye and focusing the brass tube.

He saw Count Von Falkenheim riding at the head of his men, and they looked like a small army. "It's the Diamond D!"

"Wonder what they want?" Truscott asked.

Blakemore said, "I think we'd better git ready for trouble."

"Let's not panic," Truscott said. "We ain't done nothin' wrong, and the count is known as a fair man. Let me do the talkin'."

Truscott rode to the front of his men and sat easily in his saddle, rolling a cigarette as Count Von Falkenheim and the men from the Diamond D came closer. Stone examined them through his spyglass, and they were mean-faced and grim, with the style of gunfighters.

They slowed as they approached Truscott, and Von Falkenheim's Arabian stallion danced and pranced sideways. The count urged him forward and came abreast of Truscott.

"Howdy, Count," said Truscott, taking off his hat and smiling in a friendly manner, because his best dream was someday the count would make him foreman of the massive sprawling Diamond D.

Instead, the count pulled a handful of papers out of his saddlebag and held them in the air. "I haf bought the Triangle Spur, undt I am here with my men to take the herd. I do not haf need for more cowboys, so you and your men vill haf to find something else to do."

Truscott stared at the piece of paper, disbelieving his ears. They were all fired, just like that? Stunned, he turned and looked at his men, and they didn't know what to do either. The count was one of the richest cattlemen in West Texas, with political connections all the way to Austin, and he'd bought the Triangle Spur?

But Truscott didn't want to give up the herd, because he'd put two years of sweat into it. "Who sold it to you?"

"Gideon Vhiteside."

Truscott shrugged. "He don't own it. His wife does."

"I am afraid you do not know vhat you are talking about," the count said stiffly. "In this country the husband owns the property. Now if you do not mind, get your men out of my vay."

"Count," Truscott said, "with all due respect, I think we'd better git Mrs. Whiteside, and see the judge in San Antone, and let him decide."

The count stared at him coldly. "I haf the necessary papers, and I haf paid Mr. Whiteside the price he asked. I am not going to tell you again, Truscott: get your men out of my vay."

"Sir," Truscott said, "I'm the foreman of the Triangle Spur, and I cain't give up my herd to a piece of paper."

The count's lips quivered with rage, then he turned toward his men. "Vhiteside!" he hollered.

The Diamond D cowboys made way, and a familiar one-armed figure rode among them, covered with dust, his hat dented and smudged. The men from the Triangle Spur stared at him in amazement, because he appeared twenty years older, with deep lines on his cheeks and around his mouth, and his hair whiter.

His former proud posture was gone, and he slouched in the saddle, his mouth turned down grimly as he brought his horse to a halt beside Von Falkenheim.

"Tell him!" the count ordered.

Whiteside could feel the hatred coming from Truscott and his men, but he stared into his former ramrod's eyes and said, "I've sold the ranch to Count Von Falkenheim, and I had the legal right to do it! If you're smart, you'll do as he says!"

Whiteside's voice had a reasonable tone, for the old actor was at work again, but the men from the Triangle Spur weren't moved. All they could see was the man who'd beat Cassandra before their eyes in the bunkhouse, and their hearts hardened.

Count Von Falkenheim looked down his nose at Truscott. "You heard vhat he said?"

"I ain't givin' up this herd unless the judge tells me to," Truscott replied, and behind him his men murmured their agreement.

Von Falkenheim turned to Dave Quarternight and gave a slight nod. Quarternight's face was cold and deadly as he urged his horse forward, and Truscott recognized him, a notorious gunfighter.

"We ain't got no more time to waste on stove-up cowboys," Quarternight said to Truscott. "Move yer asses out of the way."

Truscott knew he was in over his head, but a man couldn't call himself ramrod and then back down in front of his men. "Mr. Quarternight," he said, "this ain't none of yer business, and it ain't none of mine neither. I say we should let the judge make up his mind."

"I say you should move or go for yer iron," Quarternight replied.

Truscott saw the confident gleam in Quarternight's eyes, and faltered. He couldn't back down, but didn't want to die either.

"Vell?" asked Von Falkenheim impatiently. "Vhat is it going to be?"

Silence came over the crowd. The cowboys from the Triangle Spur saw they were outnumbered, and looked at each other with question marks in their eyes. Then a horse moved forward among them, and Von Falkenheim saw a tall, husky cowboy astride it. Triangle Spur cowboys cleared a path for him, and as he drew closer, Von Falkenheim was astonished to see the drunken cowboy who'd brought flowers to Veronika two mornings ago. He turned to Whiteside and asked softly, "Who is he?"

"John Stone."

Von Falkenheim put everything together in his mind, and it burned like a branding iron. He looked at Quarternight. "That is the man you vill kill."

Quarternight gazed at Stone, and was surprised by what he saw. This was no broken-down cowboy, but appearances were deceptive, and he couldn't be much if he was working for the Triangle Spur.

Tomahawk walked between Truscott and Quarternight, and Stone pulled the horse to a halt.

"Lookin' for lead?" Quarternight asked, staring Stone in the eye.

Stone looked back and didn't flinch one iota. "Get off this range!"

Quarternight thought Stone mustn't know who he was. "What if I don't?" he asked, unable to suppress a nervous giggle.

"I'll kill you."

"You'll kill me?" Quarternight asked incredulously. "You must be crazy!"

"There's only one way to find out."

Quarternight had intended to challenge Stone, but instead Stone was challenging him. Behind him, Diamond D gunfighters and cowboys moved their horses out of the line of fire, and then the cowboys from the Triangle Spur did the same behind Stone.

Stone and Quarternight, atop their horses, faced each other, only six feet separating them.

"Steady now," Stone said to Tomahawk, and Tomahawk became a statue, unblinking eyes fixed on Stone's opponent.

Count Von Falkenheim looked at John Stone, wondering if this could be the same cowboy who'd knocked on Veronika's door. That man had been a drunken slob, but this one sat on his saddle like an officer of the guards, and had an intensity that was almost palpable.

Quarternight felt it, but he'd killed sixteen men in his life, and had an intensity of his own. He angled his horse to the left, so he'd have a clear right-hand shot at Stone.

Both men stared at each other, and Stone remembered the Gypsy's curse. It was silent, and Don Emilio watched from his position near the campfire. He knew Dave Quarternight, and felt certain his gringo friend was going to die. Slipchuck also knew Quarternight, and thought Stone was no match for the gunslinger. Whiteside smiled as he watched the two adversaries from atop his horse. John Stone was the cause of his problems, and now he was going to pay.

Quarternight saw the confidence and determination on Stone's face, and felt a moment of fear, but it subsided quickly as he realized Stone was just another cowboy, with no special gunfighting skills.

"Said yer prayers?" Quarternight chided him.

"Make your play," Stone replied in a voice that was blood and steel.

Quarternight poised his hand above his gun. His horse looked at Tomahawk, and both knew one of them would carry a lighter load in a few moments.

Stone's shoulders were loose, his old cavalry hat was slanted low over his eyes, and his right hand hovered above his Colt. There was stillness, then Quarternight went for his gun.

Stone slapped his hand down, felt the gunbutt against his fingers, and yanked the Colt out of its holster. He fired just as Quarternight was taking aim, and Quarternight appeared surprised when Stone's bullet struck him squarely in the middle of the chest. Quarternight managed to pull his trigger the final fraction of an inch, his pistol fired, and the hot lead whirred past Stone's left ear.

Stone fired again, and Quarternight dropped his gun. Blood oozed out two holes in his chest, plus his nose and mouth. His face became pale, and he teetered in his saddle. Then his eyes became white and he fell to the ground.

The gunshots reverberated against distant mountains, and a cloud of gunsmoke rose in the air. Everyone stared at Dave

Quarternight, lying in a widening pool of blood. John Stone touched Tomahawk with his spurs, and steered him toward Von Falkenheim.

Von Falkenheim saw him coming, and felt stark terror. He couldn't outshoot Stone, or fight him hand to hand, but he, a Prussian nobleman, couldn't back down to a common cowboy, and particularly one who'd seduced his mistress.

John Stone came abreast of him and brought Tomahawk to a stop. "You have more men than we," Stone said to Von Falkenheim, "but if there's gunplay, many of your men will be killed, and you'll be the first to go. My advice to you is settle your problems before the judge."

"I do not take advice from *schwein*," Von Falkenheim said, and then he turned to his gunfighters, "Kill him!"

Not one of them moved. They didn't want to tangle with the man who'd shot Dave Quarternight. Von Falkenheim turned red, and his eyes bulged. "I said kill him!"

No one reached for his gun. Stone put his spurs to Tomahawk and moved closer to Von Falkenheim, who sat stiffly in his saddle. He had no one to fight for him, and didn't quite understand how that came about.

Stone stopped Tomahawk in front of him and said, "Why don't *you* shoot me?"

Von Falkenheim had no idea of what to say. If he drew his pistol, Stone would kill him. Fistfighting was beneath the dignity of the Prussian nobility, and his swords were back at the ranch.

"Get your men off this range!" Stone said.

"It is my range!" Von Falkenheim insisted, holding the legal papers in the air. "I haf bought and paid for it!"

"May I see those papers?"

Von Falkenheim passed them to Stone, who browsed through the pages quickly, then tore them into small pieces, throwing them over his shoulder.

Von Falkenheim was shocked. "Vhat you are doing!" he said. "It is against the law! There are vitnesses, undt you can be sure I vill take this up vith my lawyer!"

Stone looked at Von Falkenheim, and saw in him all the pretension, snobbery, and arrogance of his class. Stone's frustration and anger at the world crackled through his veins and became focused on Von Falkenheim. He didn't like the way Von Falkenheim had set up Truscott to be killed, or the slimy way in which Von Falkenheim tried to steal Cassandra's ranch.

Stone climbed down from his saddle, and Tomahawk stepped out of the way, because he knew something deadly would go down in a matter of seconds. Stone marched toward Von Falkenheim, and Von Falkenheim couldn't believe his eyes. It was inconceivable that someone would threaten him in this manner, but he didn't dare go for his gun.

Stone reached up, grabbed Von Falkenheim's black leather coat, and pulled him roughly to the ground. The hat fell off Von Falkenheim's head, and his baldness gleamed in the light of the sun. He struggled to maintain his equanimity as Stone set him down and pushed him away contemptuously.

Von Falkenheim tripped, nearly fell, but managed to retain his balance. Stone said, "You want this herd, you'll have to fight for it!"

Von Falkenheim looked at his men and realized they weren't going to help him. Stone had broken their fighting spirit when he'd shot Quarternight. It was a real-life demonstration of one of the oldest axioms of textbook military science: mercenaries are the least reliable soldiers.

But he was from the Prussian nobility, and courage had been bred into him. He couldn't retreat before this man.

"I see you're wearing a gun," Stone said, taunting him. "Why don't you use it?"

Von Falkenheim said sarcastically, "You are obviously an expert in this type of duel, so you haf an advantage that makes you brave, but vhat vould you do vithout your advantage, I vunder?"

Stone gazed at him scornfully, then raised his hands, turned around, and said over his shoulder. "How about now?"

Von Falkenheim looked at Stone's broad back, and was tempted to take the chance. He wasn't a gunfighter, but was certain he could shoot Stone before Stone could turn, draw, and fire.

"Go ahead," Stone said.

Von Falkenheim remembered Stone shooting Dave Quarternight, one of the fastest guns on the frontier, and one of the most expensive. Von Falkenheim concluded he shouldn't take the chance.

"No," he said, "I am not a common gunfighter."

Stone turned and faced him again, hitching his thumbs in his gunbelts. "What do I have to do to make you act like a man?"

It was a slap in the face, because Von Falkenheim valued his masculinity above his wealth or title. *I must not let him tempt me,* he thought. *I must stay calm and walk out of this alive.*

Stone took off his hat and flung it away. Then he untied his bandanna and tossed it in another direction. He unbuttoned his shirt, peeled it off, and turned his back to Von Falkenheim.

Von Falkenheim stared at the network of scratches, and it was like looking at his own back after he'd been with Veronika. His cheeks grew hot, and now the burgeoning rage swept over him. This was the deepest and most terrible insult of all, and it could only be wiped out with blood.

He raised his chin an inch, and his features became white marble. "I duel in the classical manner," he said icily. "Do you?"

"Pace off ten steps, turn, and fire on signal from the referee."

"Exactly. Vill you gif me satisfaction?"

"You bet your ass. I'll flip you for the referee."

"Beg your pardon?"

Stone tossed the coin into the air and said, "I'll take heads."

The coin landed on the buffalo grass, and Stone bent over it. "Tails. Choose somebody."

Von Falkenheim turned to his cowboys and hollered: "Fairfax!"

Don Fairfax, ramrod of the Diamond D, climbed down from his horse and walked toward Von Falkenheim. He was ruddy-faced, middle-aged, and wearing chaps and a hat with the brim rolled up on the sides. There was a worried look on his face as he came to a stop in front of Von Falkenheim.

"You are going to referee a duel," Von Falkenheim told him, and then described what he'd have to do. "Do you understand?"

"Yes, sir."

"Take your position."

Fairfax walked away, chaps flapping on his legs, and stopped midway between his men and those from the Triangle Spur. Meanwhile, Von Falkenheim turned the revolving section of his gun to make sure it was operating properly. He holstered his gun, removed his black leather coat, red bandanna, and white silk shirt, dropping them beside him on the ground.

When he walked toward Fairfax, the men could see the scratches on his back identical to Stone's. A murmur went up among cowboys on both sides of the line as Von Falkenheim came to a stop and pointed his pistol straight up in the air.

Stone walked toward him, remembering once more the Gypsy's curse. He'd never dueled in the classical manner, and maybe his time had come, but he didn't think so, and didn't give a damn anyway. All he wanted to do was put a bullet between Von Falkenheim's eyes.

The two adversaries stood back to back, their scarred flesh touching, their elbows bent and guns pointing straight up at the sky.

"Pace off!" Fairfax shouted. "One . . . two . . . three . . ."

Stone and Von Falkenheim stepped away from each other, and Von Falkenheim held his head proudly, like a Prussian officer, while Stone's chin was closer to his chest, like a prizefighter. Fairfax hollered: "Ten!" and both men stopped. "Turn around!"

Stone and Von Falkenheim wheeled and faced each other sideways, to present the smallest possible target. They gazed at each other across the dueling ground, and everybody knew one of them was going to die. Tomahawk pawed the ground nervously, because he'd developed an affection for Stone during the weeks they'd been together.

"All right, genelmen," Fairfax said. "When I say fire, you know what to do. Are both of you ready?"

"It is customary," the count said, "at this point in a duel, to offer the combatants an opportunity to apologize."

"We can skip that part," Stone replied, holding his Colt tightly in his fist, aligning his arm with Von Falkenheim, so all he had to do was bring his hand down quickly and pull the trigger.

"You may proceed," Von Falkenheim said to Fairfax.

There was a pause, and Stone and Von Falkenheim stared at each other, casting long shadows in the light of the setting sun. Hatred and revulsion passed between them as they tensed for the final word.

"Fire!" hollered Fairfax.

Both guns streaked down, and Von Falkenheim got off the first shot, but he was too eager, and his bullet flew two feet over Stone's head. Then Stone's gun fired, and Von Falkenheim was rocked back on his heels even as he was cocking his hammer for the second shot.

Von Falkenheim felt himself unraveling, and there was a terrible pain in his chest. He didn't have the strength to pull the hammer back, but with the pride of a former Prussian officer, he tried. Stone fired again, and everything went black before Von Falkenheim's eyes. He dropped his gun, wondered what mad dream brought him to this strange land, and fell to the ground, shuddered, and coughed blood.

Stone walked toward him, aimed his gun at Von Falkenheim's head, and put him out of his misery. The shot echoed across the valleys and canyons, and buzzards circled in the sky.

Stone turned toward the mounted gunfighters from the Diamond D. "Who's next!" he asked.

Nobody said a word.

"Get off this range!"

"Let's go, men!" shouted Fairfax, walking back to his horse.

The Diamond D cowboys draped Dave Quarternight and Count Wolfgang Von Falkenheim head down over their saddles and led them away. Blood dripped from Von Falkenheim's head onto the white coat of his Arabian stallion, who walked solemnly, head low to the ground, mourning the death of his master.

Stone thumbed cartridges into his Colt, as the cowboys from the Triangle Spur gathered around him, and there was new respect in their voices as they congratulated him. Stone didn't say anything, and didn't seem to hear them. He picked his shirt off the ground and buttoned it, knowing Von Falkenheim had fired the *first* shot, and if the count had held his gun an inch lower, Stone would be head down over Tomahawk, and the gypsy's curse would be redeemed.

"That was some display of shootin'," Truscott said admiringly.

Stone tucked in his shirt and put on his hat. He looked at the herd, and the cattle continued to chew grass complacently, they couldn't care less about men shooting each other.

"Can you imagine that?" young Ben Thorpe said. "They tried to steal our herd! Thought they could just ride away with it!"

Don Emilio stood nearby, his wide sombrero on his bandaged head. "Happens all the time in the brush country, my friends. That is how I and my vaqueros have come to be here ourselves."

Stone thought of Cassandra, as a mountain pierced the sun on the horizon. Her herd was safe now, because no creditors would show up in the middle of the night. They'd leave on schedule in the morning, and somehow they'd make it to Abilene. Truscott and the rest of them stood up to the Diamond D, and if they could do that, they could do anything. Cassandra would be proud of her cowboys, when she heard what they had done.

Stone flashed on the one-armed colonel who'd tried to cheat Cassandra out of her property. Stone didn't recall seeing Whiteside after the duel was over, and wondered where he'd gone. Then he remembered Whiteside smashing Cassandra in the face in the bunkhouse, and a terrible thought came into his mind.

He ran toward Tomahawk, jumped over his rump, and landed in the saddle. He grabbed the reins, spurred Tomahawk, and the black stallion leapt forward, pounding his hooves into the ground, gathering speed, as the mountains on the horizon sank into the dusk of night.

9

IT WAS DARK at the Triangle Spur, and the two women sat exhausted in the living room, a stack of boxes near the door. The windows were boarded, furniture draped with protective cloth, and tomorrow morning they'd nail shut the door. If they were lucky, maybe the Comanches wouldn't burn the place to the ground, and they could come back someday.

"I'm ready to go to bed," Cassandra said wearily. "I don't think I've ever worked so hard in my life."

"Want some warm milk?" Agnes asked.

"If it's not too much trouble."

Agnes got to her feet, a spindly old woman in a long dress and apron. "No trouble at all."

She walked toward the kitchen, and Cassandra sprawled in the big upholstered easy chair, the heels of her boots digging into the rug. She still wore her jeans and shirt, with the top two buttons of the shirt unfastened.

She felt as though the worst was over. No creditors had arrived that day, and she'd be hard to find tomorrow morning. She was going to Kansas, and someday she'd be able to tell her granddaughter all about it.

She expected it to be a grand adventure. There were rivers to cross, Indians and outlaws to fight, hailstorms, stampedes, and anti-Texas bias in Kansas, but somehow they'd make it through.

She had complete confidence in her cowboys, after the way they'd interceded for her the previous evening. She'd never dreamed that bunch of sloppy drunkards could stand up to the authority of Gideon, but they had. Underneath everything, they were decent men, and she loved every one of them. She couldn't wait to join them, and fully intended to pull her weight all the way to Abilene. She could ride, and would become one of the boys.

Her thoughts turned to John Stone, biggest surprise of all. She'd thought him a derelict who couldn't think beyond his next bottle, and he was the one who'd led the revolt against Gideon. Stone had been a different man last night in the bunkhouse. For a few moments, she'd seen the cavalry officer he must've been. God pity the man who got on the fighting side of John Stone.

She remembered Gideon, and compared him with John Stone. It seemed as though Gideon had been a bad dream, now that the veils had been torn away. Gideon was a stout old man and an obnoxious braggart, wrapping himself in the Confederate flag, using the Cause for his own dark purposes, and now she wondered if he'd ever really been in the Army at all.

She became aware of silence in the kitchen. "Agnes?" she asked. There was no answer, and Cassandra furrowed her brow. "Agnes?"

No sound came from the kitchen, and a breeze blew against the clapboards that covered the ranch house. The hairs stood up on Cassandra's neck, and she got to her feet, reaching for the gun in her holster.

"Agnes?"

There was no answer, but Cassandra was sure there was a reasonable explanation. Maybe Agnes had gone to the privy. Yes, that must be it. Cassandra eased the gun into her holster and sat in the chair.

She knew Comanches and Apaches were in the vicinity, although she'd never had difficulties with them during the two years she and Gideon had owned the ranch. There also were reports of outlaw gangs and free-lance thieves robbing banks and stealing cattle. But there'd never been problems at the Triangle Spur.

"Agnes?"

No one answered, and a chill passed over Cassandra. She glanced around nervously, and then something creaked in the kitchen. She rose and pulled out her gun. Her heart beat swiftly in her breast as she walked down the corridor, and she wanted to believe she was being foolish, because Agnes would return in a few minutes, and they'd laugh over Cassandra's panic attack.

It was pitch-black in the kitchen—why had Agnes turned out the lantern? Cassandra wanted to run, but there was no place to go and no one to hear her if she screamed. A wave of unholy terror came over her as she froze in the dark corridor.

She could return for the lamp in the living room, or continue into the kitchen and light the lamp. "Agnes?" she asked, and her voice echoed down the corridor. She decided to get the lamp in the living room, but then suddenly heard rushing footsteps coming toward her. She screamed, and something smashed into her head. The last thing she saw was Gideon's hideous face looming out of the darkness as she fell senseless to the floor at his feet.

She opened her eyes, lying on her bed. A lantern glowed atop the dresser, and her hands and feet were tied to the bedposts. The side of her head was bloody where Gideon had struck her with the butt of his gun.

He stood at the foot of the bed, light from the lamp throwing weird shadows onto his face, and his gray hair was mussed on his head; he looked like a madman.

"You're awake!" he roared, as if playing to an audience. "That's good, because I was afraid I'd killed you, but I guess your skull is too thick for that!" He laughed, filling his chest with air, his hand outstretched at his side. Then he stepped forward, grabbed a handful of her hair, and jerked her head from the pillow. "Who did you think you were when you contradicted me in the bunkhouse that night? Had you forgotten who I am, I, Colonel Gideon Whiteside, the hero of Sharpsburg? Did you think you were dealing with an ordinary man, someone who could be overcome by your idiotic smile?"

He let her head go, took a step backward, and threw out his arm dramatically. "If only you knew how much I've hated you. You never even had the brains to ask questions—you could've written to the War Department in Washington, you could've corresponded with men who'd served under General Jackson, but no, you believed every word I said, my performance was impeccable, I delivered every line perfectly. Sometimes I let you think you'd made a decision, although I had cleverly led you to it by your little nose. I have made you what you are, you are my creation, and just as I made you, I shall destroy you!"

He pulled a knife from his belt, and its six-inch blade gleamed in the light of the lantern. Cassandra screeched at the top of her lungs and strained at her bonds, while Whiteside threw back his head and laughed.

"Go ahead! Let it all out! See what good it does! No one can hear you now! We're all alone, the way a husband and wife should be alone, and we're going to make love, just as in the old days, only this time I'm going to use this!"

He held the blade before her face, and she screamed again, tears flowing down her cheeks. She could see blood on the blade; he'd cut down Agnes in the kitchen.

Whiteside filled his lungs with air and laughed, staggering from side to side, holding the back of his fist to his forehead, while his fingers gripped the gory knife.

Cassandra was so terrified she was nearly out of her mind. She tried to tell herself it wasn't happening, it was a nightmare and everything would be all right in the morning, but somehow the ropes around her wrists and ankles were too insistent, Gideon's laughter too loud, and the knife in his hand too real.

She remembered the derringer suspended by the gold chain, and wondered if there was some way she could get it. She looked at Gideon laughing at her, his eyes glittering with dementia. Somehow she'd have to outsmart him, otherwise he was going to kill her. What was his weak spot, and how could she reach it?

He struck another actor's pose. "I've been stealing from you even before we were married, and you never suspected. On many of those nights when you thought I was attending veterans meetings, I was with other women far younger and more beautiful than you, and it amused me to buy presents for them with your money, and you never even dreamed it could be happening, because you trusted me the way a sick cat trusts her mother. How poignant and immeasurably stupid, but if you'd continued to trust me, I'd have let you live. Instead you chose to humiliate me in front of those filthy drunken cowboys, and for that, my dear Cassandra, you must die!

"You see," he said in a vague singsong voice, "I've had to eat too much dirt in my life. Do you know what it is to be poor, and watch from the gutter as your betters passed, on their way to banquets, theaters, balls, and races? Do you know what it is to have a stomach hollow with hunger, and gaze through the window of a restaurant at wealthy people stuffing themselves with haute cuisine? Of course you don't know what it's like, and I guess you never will, because now, my dear Cassandra, I'm afraid your time has come. I'm going to cut your throat slowly, so you'll know you made a very great mistake when you had the audacity to rebel against me."

He advanced toward her, knife in hand, but he'd showed her his weak spot, and she homed in on it. "Gideon my darling," she said, "I've never loved anyone the way I've loved you, and if you think I should die, then go ahead and kill me. But before you do it, let me tell you about the money!"

Whiteside stopped in his tracks. "Money?" he asked. "What money?"

"Five thousand dollars! I kept it in a special account, for emergencies, and never told you about it! I drew it out of the bank today, for the cattle drive, but instead I want to give it to you, so you'll never again have to be hungry, cold, or without a roof over your head in your life!"

"Where is this money?" he asked.

"In the barn—I'll have to get it for you."

"If you try anything, Cassandra, I'll cut your throat without hesitation. You understand that, don't you?"

"Yes, but first let me give you one last gift, as a token of my high esteem, for the great sacrifice you've made for the Cause, a sacrifice that has ennobled both our lives."

Five thousand dollars was a tremendous amount of money. He saw Fate smiling again.

He sliced the ropes, and Cassandra arose from the bed. Somehow she'd have to get that derringer, cock it, and shoot Gideon. She stood unsteadily, feeling the sting of the abrasion on her head, and the ache left by the ropes on her wrists and ankles. He jammed the knife into his belt and drew his gun.

"Move," he said, pointing the barrel to the door.

She stepped toward the hallway, and turned her back to him so he couldn't see her hands as they reached to her blouse. Heading toward the stairs, she unfastened the buttons of her blouse. Gideon walked behind her, breathing like an old bull elephant, and her fingers closed around the handle of the derringer. Please God, she thought as she drew back the hammer—it made a soft click.

"What's that!" Whiteside shouted.

Cassandra spun around, her finger tightening around the trigger, and he smashed her in the face with his gun. She fell to the floor at his feet, blood oozing out of a gash on her forehead, and he aimed his gun at her right temple, then paused and recalled that he wanted her to feel every cut of the knife, *especially now.*

He holstered his gun and carried her back to the bedroom. Moving quickly, he picked up the rope and tied her to the bed roughly, because now she'd made him mad. It was the second time she'd challenged him, and the bitch had actually tried to kill him!

He walked to the dresser, picked up the pitcher, and spilled water onto her face. Deep in the black clouds, she felt liquid streaming down her face, and opened her eyes.

Gideon stood above her, the knife in his hand and his face livid with rage. "You pig!" he hollered. "You tried to kill me—Colonel Gideon Whiteside—I commanded a regiment at Sharpsburg—General Jackson himself pinned many a decoration on me—you filthy whorebitch—*die!*"

He raised the knife high in the air over her, and the room exploded with thunder. John Stone stood in the doorway, a Colt in each hand, triggering quickly, and the hail of bullets hurled Whiteside backward, his blood spraying through the air. He slammed against the wall and dropped to the floor, where he lay motionless, bleeding from six holes.

The bedroom was silent, and acrid gunsmoke filled the air. Stone, guns still at the ready, walked toward Whiteside and kicked him onto his back.

Whiteside was like a sack of flour, his eyes closed, he was dead. Stone holstered his guns and moved toward the bed, seeing that Cassandra had fainted.

He pulled the Apache knife out of his boot and cut the ropes that held her down. Then he picked her up and carried her out of the room to the guest bedroom down the hall, so she wouldn't be shocked by the sight of Whiteside when she came to.

He entered the guest room and laid her on the bed. Then he lit the lamp and found a rag, soaked it with water, and sat beside her, gently wiping away the blood. She had cuts and welts, and her hair was mussed, but somehow in the light of the lantern she reminded him of Marie. He bent toward her, and she opened her eyes when he was only inches away.

"What happened?" she asked.

"Whiteside is dead, and I think we'd better get out of here."

She arose unsteadily, and he held her arm as she staggered down the corridor. The image of Gideon was tattooed on her eyeballs, knife poised to strike. They descended the stairs to the living room. "Have a seat," Stone said. "I'll bring the buckboard around."

He went outside, and she sat on the sofa. It made her nauseous to think she'd lived with that man for more than two years, and given him everything she had.

There'd been moments when she'd doubted him, but love had overcome suspicion. I loved him too much, she thought. I didn't see what he was.

She wondered why she'd loved him so, because now she saw a preposterous old clown, false as a clay dollar, deadly as an asp. The only answer that made sense was somehow she'd transferred her love of the Confederacy to him, because he'd been able to convince her that he and the Confederacy were one and the same.

I'll never let a man do that to me again. She had a fleeting memory of making love with Whiteside on the very sofa where she sat, his one arm wrapped around her waist, and his flaccid paunch against her smooth, flat stomach.

She arose from the sofa as if it carried a terrible disease, and looked at the portrait of Whiteside over the fireplace. Hesitating a moment, she rushed toward it, took it in her hands, and threw it to the floor. Then she jumped on his face and stamped her feet.

The door opened and Stone took one look at her, then picked up some boxes and carried them to the buckboard. The full moon shone overhead, outlining the barn and outbuildings in a yellow glow. She'd almost caught him kissing her upstairs, but for a moment he'd thought she was Marie. *I've got to forget about Marie*, he said to himself, *but how can I forget her as long as Cassandra looks just like her?*

He loaded the last box onto the buckboard, and then carried Agnes's body outside, laying it behind the boxes, so she could have a decent burial on the prairie. Finally he tied Tomahawk's reins to the back of the buckboard, and returned to the house. Cassandra stood in the middle of the living room next to a pile of broken furniture and the shattered painting of Gideon Whiteside.

"Do you have a match?" she asked.

"Going to burn the place down?" he replied incredulously. "But it's a perfectly serviceable home!"

"It was the devil's home," she replied. "A match, please."

He took one out and handed it to her, and she scratched it against the wall. The match burst into fire, and she dropped to one knee, touching it to the crumpled canvas of Gideon Whiteside.

The flame traveled along Gideon's nose and attached itself to the leg of a chair. Cassandra lifted the lamp off the table and hurled it at the drapes. They became engulfed in flames that arose and clawed at the ceiling, scorching the white paint.

"I'm ready now," Cassandra said.

She walked toward the door, and he followed her outside. Tomahawk watched them approach, and could see fire behind the windows of the house. Stone placed his hands on Cassandra's slim waist and lifted her to the buckboard, then climbed beside her, grasped the reins, and flicked them.

The horses pulled the buckboard away, as swirling flames

consumed the ranch buildings. Tomahawk plodded behind the wagon, looking at John Stone and Cassandra side by side, their bodies touching, and the big yellow moon shone in the starry heavens, as they headed back toward the herd.

If you enjoyed this book, subscribe now and get...

TWO FREE

A $7.00 VALUE—

If you would like to read more of the very best, most exciting, adventurous, action-packed Westerns being published today, you'll want to subscribe to True Value's Western Home Subscription Service.

Each month the editors of True Value will select the 6 very best Westerns from America's leading publishers for special readers like you. You'll be able to preview these new titles as soon as they are published, *FREE* for ten days with no obligation!

TWO FREE BOOKS

When you subscribe, we'll send you your first month's shipment of the newest and best 6 Westerns for you to preview. With your first shipment, two of these books will be yours as our introductory gift to you absolutely *FREE* (a $7.00 value), regardless of what you decide to do. If

you like them, as much as we think you will, keep all six books but pay for just 4 at the low subscriber rate of just $2.75 each. If you decide to return them, keep 2 of the titles as our gift. No obligation.

Special Subscriber Savings

When you become a True Value subscriber you'll save money several ways. First, all regular monthly selections will be billed at the low subscriber price of just $2.75 each. That's at least a savings of $4.50 each month below the publishers price. Second, there is never any shipping, handling or other hidden charges—*Free home delivery*. What's more there is no minimum number of books you must buy, you may return any selection for full credit and you can cancel your subscription at any time. A TRUE VALUE!

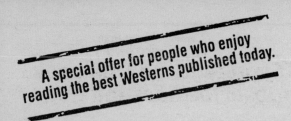

A special offer for people who enjoy reading the best Westerns published today.

WESTERNS!

NO OBLIGATION

Mail the coupon below

To start your subscription and receive 2 FREE WESTERNS, fill out the coupon below and mail it today. We'll send your first shipment which includes 2 FREE BOOKS as soon as we receive it.

Mail To: **True Value Home Subscription Services, Inc.** P.O. Box 5235
120 Brighton Road, Clifton, New Jersey 07015-5235

YES! I want to start reviewing the very best Westerns being published today. Send me my first shipment of 6 Westerns for me to preview FREE for 10 days. If I decide to keep them, I'll pay for just 4 of the books at the low subscriber price of $2.75 each; a total $11.00 (a $21.00 value). Then each month I'll receive the 6 newest and best Westerns to preview Free for 10 days. If I'm not satisfied I may return them within 10 days and owe nothing. Otherwise I'll be billed at the special low subscriber rate of $2.75 each; a total of $16.50 (at least a $21.00 value) and save $4.50 off the publishers price. There are never any shipping, handling or other hidden charges. I understand I am under no obligation to purchase any number of books and I can cancel my subscription at any time, no questions asked. In any case the 2 FREE books are mine to keep.

Name

Street Address   Apt. No.

City   State   Zip Code

Telephone

Signature
(if under 18 parent or guardian must sign)

Terms and prices subject to change. Orders subject
to acceptance by True Value Home Subscription
Services, Inc.

1-55773-620

Classic Westerns from

GILES TIPPETTE

Justa Williams is a bold young Texan who doesn't usually set out looking for trouble...but somehow he always seems to find it.

__BAD NEWS 0-515-10104-4/$3.95

Justa Williams finds himself trapped in Bandera, a tough town with an unusual notion of justice. Justa's accused of a brutal murder that he didn't commit. So his two fearsome brothers have to come in and bring their own brand of justice.

__CROSS FIRE 0-515-10391-8/$3.95

A herd of illegally transported Mexican cattle is headed toward the Half-Moon ranch—and with it, the likelihood of deadly Mexican tick fever. The whole county is endangered . . . and it looks like it's up to Justa to take action.

__JAILBREAK 0-515-10595-3/$3.95

Justa gets a telegram saying there's squatters camped on the Half-Moon ranch, near the Mexican border. Justa's brother, Norris, gets in a whole heap of trouble when he decides to investigate. But he winds up in a Monterrey jail for punching a Mexican police captain, and Justa's got to figure out a way to buy his brother's freedom.

An epic novel of frontier survival...

"Johnny Quarles brings a fresh approach to the classic western."—Elmer Kelton

JOHNNY QUARLES

BRACK

Brack Haynes knew what he wanted: a homestead of his own, a wife, and family—and peace from the haunting memories of war and bounty hunting. So he and a half-breed rancher led his cattle to the edge of Indian territory—a hostile stretch of wilderness that no white man had ever dared to claim. Everyone called Brack Haynes a crazy dreamer...and he couldn't deny it.

__BRACK 0-425-12299-9/$3.95

VARRO

Varro Ramsey's been a hired hand for the law longer than most sheriffs have been able to aim a pistol. But this time Varro wants more than cash—he wants revenge. The twisted Hall brothers left him to die in the desert, and robbed him of the woman he loves. Now there aren't enough hideouts in Texas to keep the Halls safe from Varro...

__VARRO 0-425-12850-4/$3.95